Beneath the Tor

a novel
by
Kat Yares

Beneath the Tor is a work of fiction. All characters, situations and locations came from the authors own twisted mind. Any and all similarity to real people and places is purely coincidental.

This book is dedicated to my wonderful husband, Kevin and to all those who took the Myth Class at Writer's Village University who shared the class with me and offered critiques on this work.

Prologue

I am an old woman now. The cold, damp walls of this nunnery creak around me. I smell the mildew as it clings to the stone. My sight disintegrated to a point where I see only shadows, my body frail and weak. I can no longer walk; even sitting is a chore. Although bedridden, there is one last task I must undertake before I die. I must tell the truth. I must choose a guardian of that truth. I must not let this secret die with me. However, whom? Whom shall I choose?

It can't be anyone here. These silly women have no sense of what is acceptable. Of course, it is not their fault. I blame the evangelists that Peter and Paul have sent from Asia and Rome for their failings. No longer are the teachings of the Christ taught, only the teachings of that usurper Paul. He took the teachings and twisted them and he had Peter to back him.

***

Even in her diminished state, she could still remember how she had come to be here. The high aspirations and belief in the standards she hoped to accomplish. She had been here over fifty years, since the founding of this prison for women. Originally, the ideal was that this would be a place for women devoted to the mother of the Christ, a place for spiritual enlightenment, a temple for women. Now it had become a convenience for a man to rid oneself of wives and daughters no longer wanted. A place, for most, worse than death, that allowed the Christian men to appease their own conscience that at least they had allowed them life. Very few came of their own free will, except some of the very young ones who feigned faith to save themselves from an arranged marriage, thinking that the nunnery would be more romantic and pleasant. When they learned the truth, it was far too late. Here, they too, would die.

* * *

"Bring me a scribe, child." The old woman sank deeper into the straw bed, "A young girl from the isle. There is a story I must tell before I die."

"But mother, shouldn't you be talking to one of our own girls from the nunnery?" Asked the young woman assigned to the care of the mother superior.

"Not for this story child. This story belongs on the isle. This world is not ready for it. Hurry child, do as I bid."

The young woman turned to do as she had been requested. She knew the Mother did not have much time left. In her mind, the old mother was ancient. This nunnery had been established, along with the church, back in the days when Joseph of Arimathea returned to the land. With them, they had brought a new path of faith and in the years since, had converted much of the land to this One True God. That was the story told. How the mother and at least forty others had arrived on their shores from some far off land. The old woman was the only one who knew the truth. No one else had lived as long. The oldest sister here, excepting the old woman, was only in her thirty-fourth year. There were rumors though; that the Mother had been born and bred in that pagan place called the Isle of Avalon.

"It must be true," she thought to herself, "Else why would she want a scribe from that heathen place?"

2

The young nun thought about these stories as she hurried to find a novice that could go to the isle. Only the pure of heart and innocent could venture there. Few set foot upon the isle any longer. Strangers routinely turned away, without explanation or apology.

Spying a young girl of about eight, the nun called out,

"Nimue, come here child."

The young child came obediently.

"This is very important, Nimue. Take a message to the isle. Tell them that the mother requests a scribe. Can you do that, Nimue?"

The child nodded her reply.

"Hurry, Nimue. Do not stop until you get there. Do you understand?"

Again, the child nodded.

"Then off with you." The nun said, patting the child on the head.

The child smiled, then turned and began to run though the convent. The nun watched and hoped she would get the message there in time.

* * *

The old woman looked closely at the young girl the nun ushered into the room. Dark skinned and tall, she thought, and yet she had auburn hair. Much like me. Looking closely though dim eyes, the old woman realized that this was no girl. This priestess was at least in her twenty-fifth year.

"I am Midraine, my lady. How may I serve you?"

The old woman answered quietly, "Did you bring writing utensils?"

"Aye, my lady. It was told to us you needed a scribe."

The old woman turned to the nun still standing

3

at the threshold of the room.

"You may leave us now; we will call you if we have need of you."

The nun looked startled and about to speak, then turned and left the room shutting the door behind her.

"Midraine, if you would, pull the writing table over to bar the door. Can you do that without causing yourself injury?"

"Aye, my lady." came the reply.

"My business is for your ears only. They mean well, but I have no desire or time for their comfort or meddling now."

Midraine did as she was asked, then turned to the old woman.

"My lady, why do you stay here? You are more than welcome back on the isle. We could ease your suffering there."

"My place is here now. I left the isle many, many moons ago and when I left all that was known to me was forsaken."

The old woman paused, "But now, there is a truth that has to be told and this world is not yet ready for it. That is why I sent for you. When you have this story on parchment, you must take it back with you to the isle. No one here must ever set eyes on it. When it is time, the truth will be found and revealed. Are you willing to do this?"

"Yes, my lady. Your words will go no further than my hearing. Of that you have the promise of myself, sworn to the goddess."

"Then let us begin. Much of this story I was privy and intimate with, the rest told to me by others that participated in the events." The old woman took a deep breath.

"My name is Miriam, yet the world knows me

4

as Mary Magdalene; the whore in the tale of the risen Christ. I wish to tell the truth of the events that happened over sixty years ago and reveal the secret that lies deep and quiet beneath the Tor."

Chapter One

Spring had arrived on Avalon. The oak and apple trees were bursting with buds, promising leaves of heavy green and white flowers in a few weeks. The muddy brown of the yards and gardens were showing tender shoots of grasses and herbs, beginning their life cycles anew. The pungent aroma of freshly tilled earth permeated the gentle breeze off the water.

For Miriam it was the first time she had been allowed outside since her mother's passing to the Summerland. She ran carefully through the yards, mindful of the scolding she would receive if she stepped on any of the freshly sprouting plants. Once outside of the house gardens she ran faster. As the spring wind whipped through her long auburn hair, her tiny feet carried her small frame through the debris of littered limbs dropped from the cold of the winter's cycle.

Soon she was standing at the bottom of the Tor, where Yahshua was waiting.

"A foot race to the top?" She challenged.

"You will lose this time." he replied, a smile on his face.

Miriam had already tucked her skirts and was well ahead of her cousin before he responded.

At the top, they could see the entire island. Here, they were safe from daily concerns; as seldom, except on holy days, did anyone make the steep climb.

"It seems so long since I've seen you, cousin."

"I'm glad they let you out today, Miriam. I was beginning to think they were going to keep you locked up forever." A sly smile crossed her cousin's normally somber face, lighting his deep blue eyes.

6

"They felt I needed time alone to mourn. As if I am not a trained priestess in my own right."

"I'm sure your sister did what she felt was best."

"She treats me like a child even though this will be my fifteenth summer." Miriam pouted as she fingered a new blade of grass. "Being with my mother has taught me more about life and death than most of the women here will ever know." The fire behind her emerald green eyes only hinted at the anger she felt inside.

"Let it go, Miriam. You're free now."

Miriam rolled over and let the sun flood her face. Unlike most women here on the isle, Miriam had no fear of the sun and its burning rays, her dark skin seemed immune to the pain of burning.

"I heard my father is supposed to be here today. Do you know why?"

"I do. That is why I needed to see you today. I wanted you to hear from me."

"What?" Is it something terrible?"

"We are leaving. Going back to Jerusalem."

"When? Why?" Agony filled her young voice. She felt she was now losing her best friend.

"In less than a week. I'm sure that is why Uncle Joseph is coming here today. To say his good-byes."

"But why do you have to go? You're a grown man now, you can choose to stay."

"I have been here for almost twelve years, Miriam. Studying with the Druids and learning a trade, but my family and my life are in Jerusalem. It is my destiny to go home. Or at least that is what Uncle Joseph tells me. I did threaten not to go, if you were left behind, but I don't think he took me seriously."

"I could never leave the isle, Yahshua, not even for you." The words poured from her mouth. Forced to

7

choose, she would never leave her homeland. Yet her love for Yahshua allowed her heart to break.

Tears began forming in Miriam's eyes. In three short months, she was losing everyone who mattered to her. That her father was leaving really did not matter to her. Here, unlike other parts of the world, the father of a child was not important. Here, the bloodlines ran through the mother, and only the mother could make decisions for the family. Now her mother was gone, and Yahshua was leaving too. It was almost more than she could bear. Now was not the time for tears, though, she was a priestess of the isle and she would not allow her training to be let down by not being able to control her emotions.

Looking out over the path leading to the priestesses' house, she saw that her father had indeed arrived. She knew it would not be too long before he left again, as he rarely asked to see her. In his world, girl children were worthless, only good for the alliances they could bring through marriage. Only the male child could carry on the family. How she would hate to live in a world such as his. In addition, that was what Yahshua was going back too. She wondered how much it would change him. Would she ever know? Deep down, her instincts said that she would never see him again after he left.

"So what will you do in Jerusalem?"

"I am to go study with a sect called the Essene's for three years. Then I suppose I shall take up my trade, marry, raise a family. All the usual things a man does."

"I shall miss you, Yahshua." Was all she could reply.

"I shall miss you also, Miriam. We should go down now. I am sure Uncle Joseph is going to be ready

8

to leave soon."

"This is good bye, isn't it?"

"This is good bye."

He took her in his arms then and held her close. "You will be all right, Miriam. You are the strongest woman I have ever met. Even stronger than your mother. You will make a wonderful High Priestess when your day comes."

"Cerrah is young and strong. She will be High Priestess for a very long time."

"Then, your calling will show itself. Whatever it is, I am sure it will change the future for many."

"I hope you are right, Yahshua."

Slowly, this time, they walked the winding path down from the Tor. Coming back to the house grounds, they entered the Visitors house together. No man was allowed in the priestess housing after the age of five. Entering, they could hear shouting coming from behind the closed door of Cerrah's receiving room. Both Cerrah and Joseph were arguing in very loud voices, but the wood of the door was heavy enough to muffle the words, so no one waiting in the anti-chamber could make out what was being said. Miriam and Yahshua took a place on the log benches with the other priestesses waiting. It was hours before the door opened.

Chapter Two

Cerrah walked through the door and spotting Miriam, said gravely,

"Miriam, I am glad you are here. Please come in."

Miriam felt the sting of the loss of her mother every time she looked upon her sister as Cerrah was a younger mirror image of the former Lady of the Lake. Although both herself and her sister shared the same emerald green eyes and long auburn hair, the resemblance between them ended there. Cerrah was tall, fair-skinned and carried a grace, the younger priestess could never hope to obtain.

The young priestess looked at her cousin with panic. Whatever was happening could not be good. Yahshua squeezed her hand, smiled and nodded at her for reassurance. Slowly she rose and followed her sister into the receiving room, where the massive door was once again shut tightly.

Her father, a short dark-skinned man with cold eyes, sat in a worn wooden chair in the corner of the room. Cerrah opened her mouth, as if to start to speak, when he said in a voice so stern that it frightened Miriam.

"You are to gather your belongings and be ready to leave here before dark fall, child."

"No, I am not going anywhere. I belong here. This is my mother's home. You have no rights here. No right to me."

"Be that as you will. You will be ready to go, or I will drag you forcefully from this Island. No one here will stop me." He looked at Cerrah with a defiant face;

the older priestess only bowed her head in submission.

"Cerrah, you can't let him do this." Her voice was panic-stricken, the plea obvious.

"I have no choice," was her sister's only reply.

"I don't understand."

"You don't have to understand only obey." Her fathers boomed, "Now go and make yourself ready."

Cerrah put her arm around Miriam's shoulder and whispered in her ear. "Go, Miriam. I will come and explain things the best I can in a short while. Everything will work out for the best. I do promise you that."

Miriam tore herself from her sister's embrace and ran from the room, not looking at Yahshua or the other priestesses as she fled through the anti-chamber. Safe, in her own chambers, she threw herself on the small bed, allowing the tears that had been threatening all day to finally fall.

***

As Miriam fled the room, Joseph starred coldly at Cerrah.

"You make sure she is ready to leave in an hour's time."

"Joseph, I am going to ask you again to explain why you are doing this."

"I will not tell you again, I owe you no explanation. The child is mine to do with as I please."

"No, Joseph, she is not. I have only agreed because the oracle has said it should be so. Do not think for even a moment that I fear you or that you have any power here."

Joseph glared at the young woman. Her insolence in staring back at him provoked him to speak.

"I am taking her so that I can continue to control my nephew. Have you not seen how he looks at her? He imagines he is in love." He slammed his fist down upon the arm of the chair, "If I do not take her, I doubt if he will return either. I do not want her any more than she wants to go. But Yahshua does and I am left no other choice."

"Miriam loves him also. Yet I suppose that matters little to you?"

"It matters not at all. I do not plan on allowing anything to happen between them. Once we have returned to Jerusalem, she will be of little consequence to him. He will have other matters to take up his time."

"I think you make little of their love for each other." Cerrah said quietly.

"That will change when Yahshua sees what is expected of a man in Jerusalem. He will see how foolhardy this entire situation is."

"I think your nephew will surprise you in the end."

"He will do what he is supposed to do. Now go and get the girl ready. I'll expect her in one hour's time. I've dallied here long enough, I need to go talk to my nephew."

With that, he strode out of the chamber, slamming the door behind him.

He saw Yahshua sitting on the bench in the hall. "Come, nephew."

Yahshua stood and followed him outside the center. "I have things that need to be finished at Glastonbury," Joseph said to the younger man. I want you to go on ahead to Cornwall and tell the Captain to await my arrival. I should be there in a weeks' time."

"I had thought we would travel together, Uncle." Yahshua responded.

"Matters have to be settled first. The boat will have to wait for me. Just give my orders to the Captain: Do not set sail until I have arrived. I'm counting on you to do this, nephew."

"I will do as you ask, Uncle." The younger man said. "Do you wish me to leave immediately?"

"Yes, now." Joseph barked.

"Miriam, is she all right?"

"The child is fine. Just upset, that is all. She will get over it. Now go."

"Yes, Uncle." Yahshua gave his uncle a quizzical look, then turned and started walking toward the awaiting barge on the lake.

"Yahshua, tell the bargeman to return as soon as he has dropped you on the other side."

Yahshua turned, "I will, Uncle." he replied as he continued walking to the shore.

Chapter Three

She wasn't sure how long she had been crying when she heard a quiet rap on her door. Not wanting to talk to anyone, she ignored the sound, but moments later Cerrah silently opened the door.

Barely able to open her swollen puffed eyes, Miriam asked, "Why, Cerrah, why?"

"I don't know all the answers, child. However, Joseph has convinced me that your place is in Jerusalem with him and Yahshua. I have consulted the oracles and they do agree. Just as Jerusalem is Yahshua's destiny, the goddess has determined it is yours also. Do you wish to turn your back on the goddess' will?"

"No, I would never turn my back on the goddess."

"Then go and follow your heart. I have seen how you look at Yahshua. You have always hoped to be more than friends and cousins. Maybe this is your answer, your blessing from the goddess."

"But he won't allow me any freedom with him. I have heard him talk of how it is for women in his country." The words almost spat out of her mouth. Only at this moment, did she realize that she hated the man and abhorred his ways.

"Be true to yourself and to your goddess, Miriam. Even there, allow no man to own you. You are a woman in your own right; don't let him or anyone else take that away. You can do that, I know."

Miriam smiled slightly at this. Maybe if she caused enough embarrassment for Joseph he would send her back on his next sailing ship.

14

As if reading her thoughts, Cerrah said, "Miriam, remember this, you will always have a home here. You are the next Lady of the Lake. If you return, your place will still be waiting."

"Thank you, sister."

Cerrah reached into the pocket of her robe. "Here, take this." She said, handing Miriam a small gold and amber nugget necklace. "This was our mother's, she gave it to me before she died. Wear it always. It will help keep her and Avalon close to you, no matter what the future holds."

Miriam slid the necklace over her head. "I will never forget you Cerrah, I will never forget this place. And I swear to you, by the goddess, I will never forget the lessons and training I have had here. I am a priestess of the goddess and will be so until the day I pass over."

Cerrah nodded. "Shall we begin packing your belongings?"

"What few there are." Miriam answered, her heart slightly lighter now.

Together, they folded and packed her clothing and put it in a traveling satchel. Between the layers of clothes, they put the few trinkets Miriam had collected over the years. Her gold bracelets, small seashells, her goddess stone and the small ritual dagger given to her when initiated into the mysteries. Just as they closed the small case, another knock came at the door.

"Cerrah, the man from Arimathea is here. He is asking for you. He seems very impatient."

"Tell him we are coming."

Turning to Miriam, she said, "Are you ready?"

"Yes, sister, I am."

"Remember everything we have said here. My thoughts will always be with you. You will be missed,

Miriam."

"And I shall miss you."

Arm and arm, they walked from the room and across the grounds to the Visitors house. Miriam felt her small body cringe slightly when she saw her father standing in the doorway. She forced herself to stand straighter, and when they approached closer, she said,

"I am ready now Joseph." Her voice held none of its earlier fear.

He gave her an odd look, but said nothing for a moment. Soon all the priestesses were gathered around Miriam, giving her tearful hugs and saying good-bye. One even slid her own gold ring onto Miriam's finger, adding, "It's for protection".

Joseph allowed but a brief few minutes of this, before saying, "Let us go." Leaving Miriam to carry her own bag, he started down the path to where the barge was waiting to take them back to the mainland.

"Always remember." Were the last words, Miriam heard as she followed her father down the path.

Chapter Four

Miriam struggled to keep up with the older man on the path ahead. His long strides showed he cared nothing for the young woman struggling to keep up behind him. Yet Miriam's pride refused to ask him to slow down. Upon reaching the barge, he climbed aboard and left her to her own devices. The oarsman seeing her plight, took her bag and her arm to steady her as she crossed the thin plank from shore to boat.

She tried twice to talk to her father on the short crossing. Both times, she met with stony silence. Only when they had reached the other side and walked the two miles to the inn in Glastonbury did he speak.

"You may sleep on the floor in the corner." The old man said, "I'll have the innkeeper bring up an extra blanket for a pallet."

"Joseph, I ..."

"From this moment on, you will address me as Father. No longer will I allow you to be the heathen that your mother raised you as."

"But ..."

"You will not talk unless asked a direct question. Is that understood? You will act like a proper daughter. Submissive and humble."

Miriam, so confused by her father's behavior that she could only reply,

"Yes, Father."

"I am leaving for a while. You are not to leave this room for any reason. Nor, are you to speak to anyone. The chamber pot is under the bed. I will see that you are served a meal."

With that, he was gone. True to his word, the innkeeper brought up two extra blankets and a meal of

17

cheese and bread. As she huddled in the corner, and tried to eat, she shook with fear and confusion. She had never been so miserable in her life. How dare he treat a priestess of the isle in this manner? How could her mother have ever cared for this man?

She thought of just leaving and going back to the island, yet was sure he would hold to his word and drag her away forcefully. She had nowhere else to go. She knew no one other than the priestesses of the isle. Trapped and alone she waited three empty days for his return.

When he first entered the room, his eyes went straight for the bed, as if making sure she had not slept upon it.

"I have procured the services of a chaperon for you on this journey. You are to obey her as you would me. She has my blessings to beat you into submission if need be. Prepare yourself, we sail with the morning tide in two days and must board the boat before dawn."

Miriam only nodded, her eyes cast to the floor. Meekly, she gathered her belongings and followed her father down the stairs. Rounding the corner at the bottom, a short, heavyset, grey-haired woman rose to greet them. As she walked toward them, Miriam was glad her head was bowed. She was sure her aversion was apparent on her face. The woman reeked with the smell of decay.

Miriam had been with her mother often enough on her healing journeys to know the scent of death overtaking a body from within. This woman had very little time left to live, of that she was sure. Miriam knew that she could help the woman with her suffering, but she also knew that she would not.

"This is Clandaugh." her father was saying, "You will refer to her as 'My Lady'."

"Yes, Father." came her timid reply.

To the woman, he said, "This is your charge. Keep her out of my way."

"Let me have a good look at you", the woman said, grabbing Miriam's face forcefully in her hands. The woman stared at Miriam with dark eyes, while the girl tried to keep her expression blank.

"One of the fairy folk, is she?" The woman asked her voice sounding disgusted. "As long as you do as you are told and give me no trouble, we'll have no problem. Just remember, I am not going to be taking grief from the likes of you; even if you do be a child of privilege." Her eyes burned into Miriam's with an intensity that allowed the girl to see that this woman enjoyed inflicting pain.

"I see our cart driver is here. It is time to move on. I've wasted enough time already." The impatience in her father's voice was enough to force the woman to break her grip on Miriam's face; but not enough to stop her from seizing her by the back of the neck and pushing her forward so hard, Miriam thought for sure she would fall.

Outside Miriam saw the ox cart her father had hired to take them to the coast. Extra wide, it required two oxen to pull it. The bed of the wagon was laden with goods, and Miriam wasn't sure the two animals were enough to pull the cart . Looking at the seat, she saw room for no more than three people. One look from her father told her she would be riding in the back with the rest of the baggage.

After settling into place in the wagon, the trip to the coast began without a word. Miriam found a way to shift things around to make herself as comfortable as possible. The rest of the ride before the first nightfall came was spent questioning her sister's motives. Had

19

Cerrah somehow believed that Miriam would usurp her in her position as Lady of the Lake? Is that why she had sent her away? Did Cerrah know what kind of man her father was? Had her mother even? If so, why had no one warned her? How could Cerrah let her leave the isle with no protection? At least she had her small priestess dagger, given to her upon initiation, under her mantle.

Miriam resolved that somehow she would contrive a way to get the plants and herbs she felt she needed before they sailed to this far off land. Deep within, the young priestess realized that her very survival depended upon it. Once on the boat, she would make sure that this woman could do her no harm.

Hours passed and Miriam spent the time looking at the countryside. She was watching for particular herbs and hoped that they grew this far from the isle. She knew the goddess was with her when her father finally gave in to Clandaugh's pleas to relieve herself. The wagon stopped beside a large meadow filled with spurge plants. Miriam quickly climbed out of the wagon and made her way to the nearest tree. While hidden by its trunk, she quickly gathered the vomit herb that somehow she would slip into the next meal.

Miriam knew how sick the woman was simply by looking at her yellowed skin. The herb she planned to use would cause no harm to a healthy person other than an upset stomach. Clandaugh, on the other hand, even with using small amounts, would be extremely ill, but wouldn't die from the herbs use.

It surprised Miriam how simple it was to lace the evening meal with the herb after they had made camp. When the wagon finally stopped, Miriam quietly took to the task of gathering the wood for the fire. While collecting the wood, Miriam found many other herbs to stuff in the pockets of her gown. As she had very little time, she would sort them later.

Willingly she helped prepare the meal. Heating the mulled wine her father had given for her chaperon and herself, it was easy to add the spurge to the woman's wine. Miriam watched with interest as her father drank from his own flask. The cart driver made his camp far removed from their own.

Miriam did not sleep that night, instead thought about her options. Cerrah had said that it was important that she go on this journey. In order to serve the will of the goddess, she would. Yet, not meekly. She would allow no one to harm her body, not even her father. By the time the others awoke, she already had weak tea and porridge ready for breakfast. Once again, the woman's portion was laced with the herb.

They were not an hour into the day's journey when the woman began to complain of dysentery. The wagon stopped frequently after that, yet Joseph refused to slow the pace more than necessary. He decreed that there would be no noon meal as they had lost enough time already. At every stop, Miriam took advantage of the situation and continued to fill her pockets with herbs.

At dark fall, they reached the coast. Miriam could see the ship in the harbor and said a silent prayer to the goddess hoping that she was prepared enough for what lay ahead.

Chapter Five

Miriam was tired as they loaded their belongings onto the boat. Herded to the small cabin she was to share with Clandaugh by her father, she was surprised to see that on this part of the journey she would have a bed to sleep in.

He gave instructions to Clandaugh as to when they were allowed to leave the cabin, where to go to relieve themselves and empty the chamber pot. Turning to Miriam, he said,

"You are to talk to no one aboard this ship other than Clandaugh, your cousin Yahshua, the Captain or myself. Is that understood?"

"Yes, Father," she replied. Her heart leapt for joy. Yahshua was aboard. Now she wouldn't feel so alone and frightened. She had feared he had sailed on an earlier ship.

"You may come to the deck to watch us set sail. Say good-bye to your homeland. You will never see it again."

With that said, he turned and walked away.

Miriam worked quickly to secure the few belongings that belonged to her and the older woman. The gentle sway of the boat made her movements unsteady, yet it greatly intensified Clandaugh's sickness. The older woman was now lying on her cot with her head hung over the chamber pot; her body racked with the convulsions of her heaving.

Miriam asked for and received permission to go on deck. She figured the older woman did not want to appear weak in her sickness and was glad to have Miriam out of sight.

Miriam raced to the deck just in time to see the large iron anchors hauled from the water. Going to the rail as far as possible on the back of the boat, she watched silently as the oars slipped into the water and began their stroking motions. They were underway. Helplessly the tears slipped from her eyes as she saw the shore become more distant.

Lost in her own thoughts, she did not hear the footsteps approaching from behind. Only when a hand touched her shoulder, did she become aware she was no longer alone.

"It will be for the best, cousin."

She turned and saw Yahshua standing behind her, his long brown hair gently blowing in the sea breeze. Immediately she went into his arms allowing the grief and tiredness full reign at last. She could feel his hands stroking her hair and back as a parent would a small child. It only made her sob more.

"It will be all right Miriam, I promise."

"How can you know?"

"That is one of the few answers I do know."

"Why did he make me come?"

"I fear it is because of me. I did not know he took me seriously when I refused to leave you behind. Did he not tell you?"

Miriam's heart leapt; maybe he did share her feelings after all. "He told me nothing only that I must leave. But why did you refuse?"

"Because I care for you, do you not know that? I do know you have a part to play in my destiny. Although I know not what that is yet."

"Promise me you will not go far from me when we get there. Promise me, Yahshua."

"I cannot promise you that, cousin. I already know that I will be leaving for three years soon after we arrive."

"No, Yahshua, no. I do not think I could bear
that."

"Yet, that is the way it must be. But we will
have this time on the journey. So let us enjoy, at least,
that."

***

Joseph stood on the captains deck looking at the
two figures huddled close at the stern of the boat. How
he hated bringing the girl. In the end, he felt he had no
choice. He feared Yahshua would make good on his
threat to not return with him to Jerusalem otherwise. If
he was going to continue manipulating his nephew, he
needed every game piece he could play. He felt shock
and distaste when Yahshua had told him his decision to
marry the girl. He had tried to reason with the young
man, he was of the royal line of David and he had no
business considering wedlock to a half-breed bastard
child. In the end, the only way to persuade the young
man to go to Jerusalem was to bring the girl along.
After Yahshua had finished his studies, he would be
older and wiser and know the foolishness of his
conviction.

Thank god, his own women, particularly his
first wife understood how the world worked for a man.
As Miriam was not a daughter of one of his official
concubines, she would be put in the kitchens, or even
the stables -- out of sight.

She was cunning, much like her mother, he
thought. She would need a firm hand to keep her under
control. This is why he had hired Clandaugh for the
journey. He had found her in the streets of Glastonbury
whipping a child, not even her own, for speaking in her

presence. She would keep an iron fist on Miriam until they reached their destination. Then he would send her packing.

The older man smiled to himself. The fee she had agreed on was small. Not enough for her to pay her passage back on a merchant ship. Her eyes had told him that to her mind it was riches. She would end up a beggar in Jerusalem and end up killed by the Romans due to lack of papers and under no household protection. Maybe he would leave her in Alexandria, that way she could cause him no further problems.

What mattered now, in fact the only thing that mattered at all, was that Yahshua was on the boat. They were on their way home.

If Judas and the others had followed the plan, it would not be long before Israel had their Messiah. In the more than a dozen years since he had taken the responsibility of Yahshua, he had seen to it that the boy had the education and the skills needed to defeat the Romans and reclaim Israel for the Jewish nation.

In his mind, within five years, his nephew would be crowned "King of the Jews" just as prophecy had declared. It would work, he thought, shaking away the shades of doubt. If the plan failed, then all of his effort, all his work, in fact, all of his life would have been in vain.

***

The days passed slowly and Miriam spent as much time as possible with her cousin. As the days wore on, Clandaugh continued to convulse, too ill to leave her bed.

As Miriam was cleaning up the latest mess the woman had left, her father burst through the door.

"No matter that your chaperon is too ill to care for you properly; your rules are still the same. One, and only one, minor infraction and you will lose all your freedoms."

Keeping her eyes cast to the ground, she replied, "Yes, Father."

Deep inside, she knew that she had over used the herbs and was responsible for the woman's dire sickness. A part of herself felt guilty, yet another part had no feeling at all. The older woman was mortally ill when she first came aboard and in her heart, Miriam convinced herself that she had done little to increase her suffering. She spent more than an hour in meditation, asking the goddess for her forgiveness and promising that no matter how dire her circumstance became, she would never allow her own will to stand in the way of the goddesses will again. Opening her eyes, her heart felt lighter, yet she found she was still trembling with fear. Would the goddess hear her prayer? Or would she decide that Miriam had already turned her back on what she had been taught?

Miriam could only hope for the best now. Time would answer her questions. She knew it was herself that had to have faith. Taking a deep breath, she went back to the task at hand.

***

The journey continued for what felt to Miriam like years. Her father allowed her out of the cabin only at certain times of the day, his excuse that the crew was looking lustfully upon her. Yahshua did his best to keep her time occupied, but found himself constantly at his uncle's beck and call.

They were approaching Alexandria. Miriam could overhear the crew talking about what would happen when they reached shore. Most of the crew had been frightened when Clandaugh had stayed so ill. Miriam wondered curiously, where the idea had come from that a woman aboard a ship was bad luck. At times, she had to smile when she thought about how the crew was going out of their way not to look at her, let alone speak to her in light of her father's ravings.

Three nights before reaching port, Yahshua slipped into her cabin, carrying a tray of dried fish and fruit.

"I heard Uncle Joseph confined you to your cabin. Have you eaten?"

Miriam looked at the food as if it was ambrosia from the goddess. Clandaugh had recovered enough and had left her to go on deck for fresher air. Her confinement had been the punishment for looking her father in the eyes yesterday. She had not eaten since.

"He'll disown you if he finds you here." she said.

"He's busy with the captain. Laying down orders about his cargo. No need to worry. Eat."

Eating at first like a wolf cub that had not had food since summer, slowly she began to slow down and enjoy the meal in front of her.

"Is he always like this?" she asked.

"He is a hard man. You cannot change him from the course of what he feels is right and wrong. I know, I have tried."

"He scares me, Yahshua. I am afraid he would just as soon wish I were dead. What am I going to do, Yahshua? How will his family greet me? You know them, tell me what you think."

27

"His family is going to hate you. His son's Judas and Barabbas especially. They will make life very hard for you. His wife will see only that you are proof of his infidelity."

"Infidelity? You mean a man is to sleep with only one woman?"

"No. A man is permitted more than one wife. However, she must be Jewish. He is allowed concubines, if he can afford them, but his first wife has rule over them. Martha did not have that over your mother."

"You only make my fear grow. Is there no one in this place who will make me feel welcome?" Miriam said, the tears in her eyes brimming and falling down her cheeks.

Yahshua held his arms out to her and she went into them.

Before the night was over, she was no longer a virgin priestess, but a priestess full born.

By the time they reached Alexandria, Miriam knew she carried Yahshua's seed in her belly. Her father would no doubt beat her to death, but she was so happy not to be alone that she didn't care.

Chapter Six

Miriam watched as the ship made dock. Everything was ready for debarking; she was just waiting for her father's orders. They came within an hour of mooring. Allowing Clandaugh to lean upon her, they made their way from the cabin to the ladders dropped over the ship side into small boats. Miriam waited while Clandaugh slowly made her way down the ladder, hoping that if the woman fell, someone would catch her. When Clandaugh was safely in the boat, Miriam stepped her way down the ladder.

The boat had anchored as close as possible to the Egyptian shore. Miriam could see the tall monuments and obelisks rising in the air within the city of Alexandria. The small boats wasted no time getting their cargo to shore. Miriam helped Clandaugh from the boat. Her father stepped out next.

Taking out a small leather pouch, he threw it at the feet of the older woman.

"Your services are no longer needed. There is your pay."

Clandaugh looked at the man as if in shock. "Where am I to go sir?" she asked.

"That is not my concern." came her father's reply. Grabbing Miriam by the arm, he led the small party away from the shore into the city.

The camel ride from Alexandria to Jerusalem was uneventful. Miriam spent every moment possible at Yahshua's side, basking in the love she felt for him. She didn't tell him she was carrying his child. She knew there was a possibility that it was all wishful thinking on her part. She would wait until she missed

29

her monthly courses before she shared the news.

As they approached Jerusalem, Yahshua told her of the plans that had been made for him.

"Miriam, after we reach the city, I'll not see much of you. As I told you on the Isle, I am being sent away to study. It's not a thing I want to do, but I have my obligations. I'm not deserting you. I would be with you if I could."

Miriam could not speak, only bite her lip. She had tried to forget he was going away. She had pushed from her mind, all thoughts of being alone here in this new land.

"The Goddess will protect you Miriam. I know you have a part in this and I know it is good and pure. Hold to your faith. You have my love and her protection, nothing can truly harm you here."

Her father interrupted further conversation.

"Put on your veil, girl. A woman is not seen on the streets of the city of David without one. Do you think I want you taken for a whore?"

Miriam affixed the veil over her face as her father instructed, wondering how a woman could be thought of this way. On the isle, only during certain rituals were the priestess's required to wear robes and hoods covering themselves. Any other time, they wore their gowns or nothing at all. Why were men, like her father, so ashamed of the female form?

The city gates were just ahead and she could hear the hustle and bustle of people. All around her were men, dressed as her father and other men who wore the uniform of the Roman army. There were many women in the market once they entered the gate, most covered from head to toe. Occasionally Miriam would spot a woman in cooler clothing, wearing no veil. They were of lighter skin and Miriam assumed these must be Roman women. Behind her veil, Miriam frowned and thought. *Why couldn't my father had been Roman?*

Joseph stopped the caravan in front of a large stable. Quickly dismounting, he began barking orders at everyone in sight. Yahshua helped Miriam from her camel. They both stood and waited. Yahshua leaned down and whispered into Miriam's ear,

"We are not far from your father's villa. Be ready."

"I do not think I'll ever be ready." she replied.

Within moments, Joseph tossed her small traveling bundle at her feet.

"We walk from here."

Miriam couldn't help but notice that neither Joseph nor Yahshua carried anything. Servants followed behind them, carrying bags and other items from the caravan.

As they wound through the streets of Jerusalem, unfamiliar scents and odors assailed her. The narrow roads were dirty, littered with refuse, rotted food and feces. The whole city had a disgusting stench. Watching people as she walked, she soon understood why. Men here urinated and defecated alongside the roads, wherever the urge hit them. Somehow, Miriam knew women did not have that luxury. Food scraps were almost everywhere in the streets and beggars and street urchins inspected them all in search of a bite to eat. How could these people ignore those worse off than they were? How could her father, and even Yahshua, be so blind to the suffering around them? Looking into the eyes of a small child with a distended belly, she wondered if the temples took care of the poor such as these.

Miriam followed her father through the carved

doorway of his villa. Unlike the other homes she had seen along the way, Joseph lived in a home of Roman style. At first entering the outer gardens, he looked at her and said,

"Stay here until I come for you," he then looked at his nephew, "Come Yahshua, I am sure there is a meal waiting for us. "

"No, Uncle. I will stay with Miriam. When she is settled, then I will eat."

"As you will." came Joseph's reply. Miriam could tell by the look on his face he was angry.

"He hates me." Miriam said.

"No. Not really. No more than he hates all women. You must understand Miriam, in this culture woman is to blame for all life's ills."

"All of them? What do we do that is so terrible?"

"Nothing. Just an old Hebrew folk tale many take seriously."

"Is that why I feel like I am nothing more than a tarnished trinket to him?"

"Unfortunately, in his eyes, that is all you are. I'll do what I can to protect you, but Miriam; you are going to have to help yourself. Do what you need to do. Life will be hard, but the day will come that my studies are ended and I'll be here."

"Not soon enough, I fear." she said, attempting a smile but not succeeding.

The daylight was fading from the sky and Miriam wondered how long they would be kept waiting here. As the twilight blended into full darkness, finally she heard footsteps on the cobbled stones.

"Nephew, it is very good to see you again." A feminine voice rang out.

Yahshua rose and kissed his aunt on the cheek.

32

"You, also, Aunt Martha."

"So, you're the daughter? I always wished for a girl child. But you're too dark and ugly. I could never pass you off as a relation of mine."

The woman who stood before Miriam was tall and graceful. Not as dark-skinned as her father, yet had the same dark hair. Although Jewish, she was dressed in the airy Roman clothing. Her hair braided around her head, she wore no veil only an ornate gold brooch in her hair. Miriam supposed she was pretty in her own culture, yet the woman was too coarse-looking to have been so in her own.

"Aunt Martha, that was a cruel thing to say." Yahshua said quietly.

"Cruel, possibly, but true. I don't know why he brought her here, but I have been told it is here she must stay until other arrangements are made. I will not have her thinking she will be treated as anything special here. She is an embarrassment to me."

"I'm sure you'll think of some way to save face, Aunt. Now, can you find it in your heart to feed Miriam and give her a bed to sleep in?"

"Come along, girl. I'll show you to your bed. I'll have one of the servants bring you something to eat. Maybe by morning, I'll know what's to be done with you."

Miriam uttered her first words of the conversation, "Thank you, my Lady."

"Don't thank me. Thank your cousin. As far as I'm concerned, you could sleep in the doorway."

Miriam bit her lower lip. She was not going to allow this woman to see her cry. When she was alone, then she would allow her tears. For now, she drew upon her inner strength and forced her emotions into place.

33

Yahshua stood and extended his hand to Miriam. Taking it, she rose to her feet. With Yahshua still holding her hand, they followed Martha into the villa. Miriam was not surprised to see the signs of her father's wealth as they passed through the halls. Only as they reached the back of the villa did she feel shocked. Her father's servants lived in tiny quarters, sharing them with chickens and other small animals. Although her head was bowed, she tried to repress the tears that welled up in her eyes from the compassion she felt for the way her father treated them. At the end of a long hallway, Martha stopped and pulled a tapestry back from a doorway.

"This will be your chamber. See that you stay in it until you are called." The older woman turned and walked away.

Miriam ducked and went into the room. At least there was a bed. The only other furnishings in the room were a small table and chest. Miriam hoped that she would be able to secure a candle or a lamp, as the room had only a small window that even in the brightest sunshine would not illuminate the room. Yahshua set her carrying bag on the bed.

"I'll see if I can find you something to eat." he said, with a smile. "You must be half starved."

"I am."

"I'll be back as soon as I can."

True to his word, Yahshua returned carrying a tray laden with dried fruits and fresh vegetables. Along with the food, he had secured a small oil lamp to lighten the darkness of the room. Together they ate what would be their last meal together.

"I will be gone before you awaken in the morning, Miriam. You will be all right, I promise you that."

"How can you promise that? You will not be here." Anger crept into Miriam's voice.

"I have talked to Uncle Joseph and he has promised he will be kind to you."

"It is obvious I am unwanted and unwelcome."

"It was my love that brought you here. I am sorry, Miriam."

Miriam's heart rose. He loved her. Now she knew. Nothing would be too much to bear now that she had that knowledge.

"And you promise you will return to me in three years?"

"You can begin planning our marriage if you wish." he smiled at her, then added, "But I wouldn't mention it to Uncle Joseph or Aunt Martha. They feel they have the plans for my life worked out and I don't think they have included you. I think they hope that by my being away, I will forget. Then they will send you back."

He took her into his arms. "I won't forget, Miriam. I have loved you since I was a child. Once this duty is fulfilled, nothing will keep me from you."

Miriam smiled and leaned against her betrothed shoulder. Feeling safe in his arms, she allowed her eyes to close and was soon asleep.

Miriam woke as daylight began streaming through the tiny window. Yahshua's cloak still gently tucked around her body. She could still smell him near her. Within moments of sitting up from the bed mat, a servant entered the small room.

"They are awaiting you in the salon, miss."

Miriam quickly stood and began trying to tidy herself.

"If you'll follow me, I'll show you the way." The young servant said softly.

Miriam entered a large room with a long table that looked as if it would collapse with the weight of the food that was upon it. More than a dozen people were present and she looked around wildly hoping that Yahshua was among them. Breathing a sigh of relief, she walked over to a man standing with his back to her.

"Yahshua. You are still here."

The man turned and disappointment filled her face.

"So you're the bastard sister." the man said.

Miriam was at a loss for words. This man could be the twin of her beloved. Yet where Yahshua's features were soft, this man's were cold and hard. Instead of the brilliant blue eyes that she could lose herself in, this man had eyes that were near black, like cold slate. She stammered an apology.

"Forgive me sir, I mistook you."

"Well at least you appear to have some manners."

She bowed lowly and backed away. Everything in her wanted to run. As she carefully stepped backwards, she heard him say,

"I could be a rich man in my own right if I could be paid for every time I've heard that in the last day."

Miriam realized that everyone was looking at her. Keeping her head bowed, she glanced at each person in turn. Her father was not yet in the room. His wife Martha however was. Standing near the table looking at her with sheer hatred scowled upon her face.

Miriam wished that she could hide. Never in her life had she sensed emotions such as these. On the isle, everyone was treated with respect, both by those who lived there and those in the outside villages where they visited.

The man who resembled Yahshua continued to stare at her. His stare made her more uncomfortable than the hatred of Martha, as his eyes were filled with both contempt and lust. He, more so than her father, frightened her.

She did not dare leave the room to flee back to her small cell. Straightening her back, she gathered her inner strength and began staring back. The minutes passed slowly and one by one, the occupants of the room went back to their conversations. Except for the wife and the man. Occasionally they would exchange glances at each other, but for the most part, they kept their eyes on Miriam.

The door to the salon opened and she watched her father enter the room. Once again, the conversations silenced. Everyone turned to look at Joseph.

'Has everyone's curiosity been satisfied?" He asked, grinning as he reached for a handful of dates from the table.

The questions began immediately. Miriam could only stand and fume as they talked about her as if she were invisible. Her father explained why she was there - he would not allow a child of his to remain a heathen. Soon afterwards, the questions began to lull as people began filling their plates and eating.

"Where shall you put her?" Joseph asked, turning to his wife. "She needs to be busy to keep her out of trouble."

"I think the kitchens. One of the pantry servants has left and she can earn her keep there." Martha looked at Miriam with a hint of a smile that the young woman knew was not in kindness.

"Besides, I never want to see her face again. Promise me once again that you will find other arrangements for her soon."

"As soon as I have the time to find suitable housing for her." he answered.

Joseph walked over to Miriam and said quietly in Celt, "You have heard the wishes of your mistress. Take yourself to the kitchens and tell them you are their servant. Do not show your face when any of us visit there for any reason. Now go."

Miriam forced herself to keep her composure as she walked from the room. Once in the hallway, it was all she could do to keep from running from the laughter that followed her out the door.

Chapter Seven

Judas sat in his bedchamber mulling over the day's events. He could not remember his mother being so angry, yet he felt a kinship with the young woman his father had brought back from his latest journey to the isle. One look at the girl and Judas had known immediately where his true roots lay also.

Barabbas had teased him unmercifully when they were children about being a bastard child of their father. Judas had known his whole life that there was no way he could be a full-blooded Jew, his very features denied that possibility. But until now, no one would talk to him of his true parentage, and he had always assumed that he had been an unfortunate brought into the household by Martha, the woman he knew as his mother.

Seeing Miriam, and seeing the same red hair, the green eyes and the small stature told him he too came from the isle. Did they share the same mother? It was a question he could ask neither his father nor his mother. There were so many questions, he wished now he could ask someone.

Why had Martha been so accepting of him and yet, despised the girl on sight? What was his father's true purpose in bringing the girl here to Jerusalem? It was obvious that she had not come of her own accord, even with her obvious feelings for his cousin, Yahshua. What was Yahshua's role in all of this? Judas knew his father had some secret great plan for his nephew, but Judas had been privy to only a few minor details.

The thoughts played in his head as he laid back and tried to sleep. Each question led to another until finally his head was swimming. Ringing the small bell by the bed, he waited for a servant to knock on the chamber door. The call answered and fulfilled, Judas poured a cupful of strong wine and downed it in one gulp.

Filling the cup a second time, his thoughts returned to Miriam. Was she indeed his full sister? Would she be willing to talk about where she had come from, who her mother was and possibly answer the many questions he had?

Judas resolved to show kindness to the young woman. He knew the household staff had already gossiped about her parentage and of Martha's banishment to the kitchens. He hoped his father would indeed find somewhere else for her to live, as his father's daughter she deserved to be treated better than a common slave.

* * *

Miriam soon fell into a routine in the kitchens. In many ways, she found the small pantry room to be a sanctuary from the rest of the household. She had been given the job of kneading the bread dough for the many loaves needed each day to feed a household of such size. Listening to the gossip of the other servants, she soon discovered that over twenty people called the villa home. All were relatives of Joseph and Martha. The man who looked so like Yahshua was their son, Barabbas. None of the servants liked him, preferring Judas' kinder approach to his brother's leering and lustful ways.

No one here talked directly to her, yet many talked at her. A few of the servants had taken pity on her because they knew the truth of her parentage. The

40

others treated her as the remainder of the house did; less than a servant, little better than a slave.

The weeks passed slowly with Miriam getting to her cell long after dark and rising well before dawn. Although she was used to hard work, Miriam found herself exhausted. She supposed it was because of the child she carried inside her. So far, no one had questioned her about anything personal, so she knew her secret was safe for a while longer.

Five months went by, one day bleeding into the next until she no longer remembered exactly how long she had been here. As she dragged herself to her cell after a particularly hard day, she was surprised to find Barabbas waiting there for her. It was obvious to her that he was drunk on wine.

"Did your mother look like you?" he asked.

"Yes, she did." Miriam answered, afraid not to.

"I can't imagine why my father was attracted to her. That red hair is absolutely offensive."

Without waiting for a reply, he lunged at her, grabbing her roughly by the arms.

"But maybe your kind is better in bed than our own women are." He said, throwing her onto the small bed.

Miriam wanted to scream, yet knew it was useless. There was no one here that would come to her aid. Choking back the revulsion she felt, she tried to push him away as he fell on top of her.

"Stay still woman or I will make this worse for you."

The man's hands were all over her, finally settling for using one to push up her tunic. Suddenly he pushed her away.

"You're with child!" he screamed.

Miriam closed her eyes. There was no telling

what would happen to her now. Barabbas rose quickly from the bed. Grabbing her by the throat, he yelled,

"Who is the father of this child? What man would dare touch you here in this house?"

Miriam refused to answer. Even when he began slapping her face, she kept her secret behind closed lips. He moved away.

"Father will kill you." He said as he pulled the tapestry away and went through the opening.

Hours later, she heard them screaming at each other. The high-pitched voice of Joseph's wife calling her a whore. Barabbas must have woken them from sleep to tell them the news. They were arguing now about what was to be done about her.

"The whore will not spend another night in this house. Imagine, carrying a child and refusing to tell who the father is. Probably a Roman soldier."

"Martha, calm down. I will find a place for her. She will be out of your way soon."

"She will be out of my way before daylight. I will not have her in my house another day."

"Let me go visit Mary in Nazareth. I should have thought of that before. I am sure she will take her in."

"You can visit who you want. You were supposed to take care of this matter months ago. The girl can sleep in the leper pits tonight for all I care."

"Would you allow me a week if I find who the father is?"

"She's too clever. You'll not get that out of her."

"I will beat it out of her if I must. My purpose in bringing her here was not to play the harlot."

42

Chapter Eight

The fight raged on and Miriam wasted no more time. From the corner of the sleeping quarters, she pulled her small bundle of personal possessions. Wrapping herself in Yahshua's cloak, she quietly made her way out of the plaza. Not knowing anyone here, she had no idea of where to go. As she wandered the streets of Jerusalem, she was struck by the amount of poverty she saw. Even in the darkness, children ran naked, their bodies covered in sores. Women and children alike searched beneath the empty peddlers' carts for crumbs of bread or cheese. Cripples sat in most every doorway with their mat and cup, looking for sympathy that no one seemed to give them. Miriam pulled her belongings closer to her. Winding the lanes that were only wide enough for a single chariot, she eventually came to a roman temple.

The statue of Caesar stood to the left of the doorway and to the right was a sculpture of an unknown goddess.

"Can she be here in this place?" Miriam asked aloud. Glancing around to be sure she was not seen or followed by her father. Making the decision, she almost ran up the stairs.

Entering the doorway, she was first taken aback by the size of the temple. Ornate statues of the goddess in her many forms stood full size around the perimeter of the room. As she stared in wonder, she was not aware that another person had joined her.

"I believe you must have entered here by mistake." A soft feminine voice said.

Miriam swirled around as if she had been

struck. Before her stood a beautiful, fair-haired woman of medium height with flesh as light as alabaster, dressed in a white tunic with a blue mantle woven with fibers of gold and red.

"No, ma'am. I think this is the first time I have truly felt I was somewhere I belonged since I came to this vile country."

"You're not a Jew then?"

Miriam pushed back the veils from her hair and face.

"My mother was Keltoid."

"And your father?"

"My father is dead to me as I am to him."

"This is the Temple of Isis. You are welcome here as long as you earn your keep. Have you any talents?"

"I am a priestess of the Isle of Avalon. I am skilled in the use of herbs and plants. I can read and write in Kelt and Hebrew and speak the language of most of the merchants that visited. I can also do most domestic duties."

"We can use your skills here. Come, let us find you a bed."

"First there is something I must tell you. I am with child."

"That is nothing to me, provided you keep up with your duties. When is the child due?"

"In approximately four moons."

"Then you have plenty of time to fall into the routines of your duties as a neophyte here." The older woman's eyes sparkled as she smiled.

"Thank you Priestess."

"I think I will have much to learn from you also. Tell me about this Isle of Avalon. Where is it? Is it part of the Roman Empire?"

They walked toward the back of the main temple and through an opening leading into a hallway.

"No, Priestess. I had never seen a Roman until I came here. We are all Keltoid there, except for the occasional tin trader or merchant."

"And your father was one of these?"

"Yes. He was a tin trader."

They had reached a small room at the end of the hallway. Inside were several bed mats, and a small wash table.

"This is where the neophytes sleep. You must be weary. I'll send Ariade to you to show you which mat is to be yours. We will talk more in the morning. Finding you in the temple was such a surprise, I forgot to ask your name."

"Miriam." she responded, her head bowed

"Miriam, I do hope you'll be happy here. I think we have much to teach each other. And child, you do not have to bow to me, only to the Goddess."

"Thank you, Priestess." Miriam felt her heart lift and for the first time began to believe she might find a haven here after all.

True to her word, soon after the priestess left a young woman entered the room, carrying a tray with bread, cheese and wine.

"Hello Miriam and welcome. My name is Ariade. Here, take this mat beside mine. I feel we are to become great friends. I too, am a long way from home."

The young priestess was no taller than Miriam herself, yet had a yellow tone and shiny straight black hair.

Miriam felt overwhelmed at the welcome and could think of nothing to say, only nod.

"Come eat. You must be famished."

"Yes, I am." she finally stuttered.

"Then eat. I'll talk."

Miriam sat on the mat and began to break the bread. "Are you not joining me?"

"No, that is your meal. The rest of us have already eaten. The priestess said you were with child and were to be given extra."

The meal on the tray was more food than Miriam had seen since that last meal she shared with Yahshua. Once she began eating, she realized how starved she really was. As she ate, Ariade began telling her of her own home the Far East and how she came to be in Jerusalem.

As Miriam listened to her story, she began to put her own self-pity aside. Kidnapped from her home as a young child and sold to slave traders, she served many masters before being sold to an old Ivory trader. Travelling by caravan to Jerusalem for the markets, he died after reaching the city. The High Priestess, Mircalla, had found Ariade wandering the alleys, bruised and near naked, in search for food and brought her to the temple.

***

As the months passed, Miriam found her work at the temple hard, yet satisfying. Her belly grew with the child and other than a mild backache at the end of each day, she had no reason to complain.

"Ariade, it is my time, the water has rushed." Miriam called out as she felt the liquid gush between her legs. Although not in pain yet, she carefully stood up from the table where she had been transcribing holy documents from Roman into Hebrew. Carefully she made her way to the room that had been made ready for

46

the birth. Ariade was right behind her.

"Should I fetch Mircalla?"

"No, there is no need to disturb her yet. I feel no pains so I fear it may be hours before this child chooses to appear. Will you stay with me?"

"You know I will, Miriam." the Asian girl replied. "Are you afraid?"

"Not afraid, anxious yes. I will be glad to be delivered." Patting her stomach, she continued, "This has become a heavy burden the last few weeks."

"Will you foster the child out as Priestess Camilla has done?"

"No!" Miriam said sharply. "This child stays with me."

"You must love the father very much, to already be so attached to the child."

Miriam could only smile. No one had asked her who the father was. Here, like back on the isle, paternity meant little. Only to her father and his family would it be such a disgrace.

She lay back on the pallet and thought again of her father. While she still hated him, she realized that the hate no longer filled her mind. Since coming here, she had heard nothing from him, although she feared she had been recognized by some in the market and who told him of her whereabouts. Miriam was sure that his wife was happy and relieved that she was gone. Her father was gone on business often enough that it was of little consequence.

Chapter Nine

The child was born a full day later. Miriam named her Vivienne after her mother. Within days, she was back working light duties within the temple. Another year passed and Miriam discovered she was happy. She had her work and she had her daughter. She missed her former homeland but rarely allowed herself to think about it. Instead she kept herself busy teaching the younger neophytes how to read and write. Very few of the women who came here had that skill, mostly because of patriarchal attitudes about educating women. Mircalla insisted on, and Miriam agreed, that all women should have the knowledge to read about the world around them.

More so now, since Vivienne's birth, Mariam seldom left the temple. Deep inside was the fear that if found, her father would drag her back to his household imprisoning her forever. Never had Vivienne seen the world outside the temple. There would be time enough for that when she got older and was made to understand the dangers of living in this place. Occasionally, Miriam would catch herself thinking of how different it would be raising the child in Avalon, yet she knew that no one could love the child more than the priestesses and neophytes here. Everyone took a part in her care. One old priestess had assigned herself as Vivienne's guardian and would stay in the children's room with her all night long, standing guard.

The sound of crashing stone caught Miriam's attention as she peeled the vegetables for the evening meal. Ariade ran into the kitchen, grabbing Miriam by the arm pulling her into the panty. Frantically, she pushed foodstuffs aside as she reached behind the shelves. A hidden door in the far wall opened. She pulled Miriam inside the door and shut it quickly.

"What is going on?" Miriam demanded.

"They are looking for you."

"Who is looking for me?"

Ariade put her finger to her lips, "Shush, not so loud. It is the Roman soldiers. Your father has sent them."

Miriam's heart fell. "Vivienne. Where is Vivienne?"

"Do not worry, she is being hidden also."

"But why? After all this time."

"I do not know, Miriam. All I know is that we must stay here until Mircalla tells us it is safe."

Miriam slid down against the wall. Why now, why couldn't he just leave her alone?

It was hours before Mircalla came to them. By then Miriam was more confused than ever and the older priestess tried to tell her what she knew.

"Your father wants the child. The search was not meant for you. But he intends to have the child."

"Why would he want Vivienne?" Miriam asked.

"I do not know. But I think I have convinced the soldiers she is not here. That she died in birth. You have never taken her out of the temple, so no one should be able to dispute that."

"What am I going to do, Mircalla?"

"We have to get the child away from here. Is there someone, anyone you could send her to?"

"The only place she would be safe would be back on the Isle. I know Cerrah would protect her. But I have no money for that."

"We'll work something out, don't worry, Miriam." Mircalla smiled.

"It is dangerous for you with me being here, isn't it?"

"No, I do not think so. Your father, with his contacts, surely has known you were here all along. If he wanted you, I feel sure the soldiers would have asked for you. Now come, your child is hungry."

Miriam left the small enclosure and almost ran to the children's room. Vivienne was sitting on the floor, playing quietly with a wooden block. Miriam picked the child up and held her close, allowing her to nurse.

It broke her heart knowing that she would have to be sent away. But she wasn't going to allow her father to have the child. As the child suckled, she tried to think of another option and came away with none. She had no idea of how to reach Yahshua, she didn't even know where he was. It was still more than eighteen months before he would return. Yet how would she come up with the money needed to send the child back to the isle.

Soon, the child was asleep in her arms. Miriam stood and carried the sleeping baby over to her mat and laid her on the bedding, covering her with a light blanket. Satisfied she was asleep and seeing the older priestess sitting in the corner standing guard, Miriam left the room for her own quarters.

Miriam sank cross-legged onto her own mat. At its side was a small basket holding her few personal possessions wrapped in a cloth bundle. Unwrapping the cache, she made a mental inventory of what was there. Four silver bracelets, one inlaid with semiprecious stones of the isle, several gold rings, and the silver and amber necklace that Cerrah had given her of her mother's when she had left the isle.

She made a decision to send Ariade to the

market tomorrow to see if she could find a buyer for the items. The gold ring she wore on her finger was given to her for protection and now it would buy the protection of her daughter. The same with the other treasures, their bounty would help to pay for the chaperone who would accompany her daughter home. Her mother's amulet, she would try to keep if only to save for her daughter.

Miriam prayed it would be enough. She would ask Mircalla for help tomorrow. She knew she would not be able to make these arrangements herself, that would only confirm to the authorities that the child was still there. Miriam closed her eyes and asked the Goddess for guidance. As she meditated, tears streamed down her cheeks.

Another thought entered her mind. Mircalla had suggested it in the past, yet she had refused. Now, things were different. Yahshua had even told her to do what she had to do to survive. Now she would.

She would entertain the male visitors to the temple. It would have been expected of her on the isle and she felt even here the goddess was guiding her. Unlike the Jewish women in the city, Miriam had no shame of her body or the pleasures it could bring to a man. Although she had not practiced it with Yahshua on the boat, she did know how to protect herself from becoming with child. With all these thoughts firmly in her mind, she went to talk to Mircalla.

A fortnight later, Miriam kissed her daughter good-bye and handed her to Ariade. Hugging the young woman who was her best friend, she said,

"Keep her safe for me."

"I will guard her as if she were my own, I promise you that Miriam."

"I know you will. I wish the protection of the

51

Goddess around you on your journey."

"I will return as soon as I can."

Miriam reached up, removed her mother's amulet from around her neck, and hung it around the neck of her friend.

"Keep this for Vivienne when she becomes of age. Show it to Cerrah, so she will know the truth of your claims. If you choose to stay, I will understand. Cerrah will welcome you. Vivienne will need you for some time to come as her whole world is changing and she is too young to understand."

"This cannot be good-bye, I at least will try to send word."

"I will await it. But we cannot know what the future holds. Maybe Cerrah and the Oracle can shed some light on that. Give my sister my love and warmest thoughts. Now go, the caravan leaves at dawn and you need to be ready."

"I will do all you ask, Miriam. I will not let your daughter forget her mother."

A last hug and a last kiss for Vivienne were given and the young neophyte turned and left. Miriam wept silent tears as she watched her form disappear into the crowds of Jerusalem, wondering if she would ever see her child again.

Chapter Ten

Joseph stood near the temple of Isis, contemplating his next move. The old woman Clandaugh had followed him here to Jerusalem. He had almost run over her in the market. When she had looked up, she recognized him and begun her campaign to extort more money.

"I hear the little tart is now a prostitute in the temple." she had begun.

For a few moments, he couldn't place the woman, but the minute she spoke with the accent and language, he knew.

"I do not know what you are talking about woman. Get away from me." he answered in her own language.

"Your daughter sir, the one you forced to come. She's servicing men in the Temple of Isis."

"I have no daughter." He replied as he looked around to see if anyone were watching.

"Aye, you do, sir. I'm sure she is a shame to you."

"I have no daughter." he repeated.

Only his family that lived inside the villa knew of her existence. Fear of losing his support and grace, they each kept silent rather than face his wrath.

"I know that's what you wish everyone to believe. How terrible it would be for you sir, if it were to come out what she is doing. A disgrace to a man of your stature."

The brazenness of the woman appalled him. How dare she threaten him?

"What would it take for your silence?"

"A few gold coins sir. Nothing you could not

spare. But I have not eaten anything but crumbs for days and my belly is very empty."

Joseph had reached into his leather purse, and with practiced fingers withdrew two gold coins of small value. He held them up before her eyes,

"And what promise do I have that you will say nothing?" he asked.

"You have my word sir." The old woman gave him a toothless smile as reassurance.

He handed her the two coins,

"Leave here; don't let me find you again."

"You have my word, sir."

Joseph watched as she took the coins, hiding them in her bosoms. He would have to do something about her. As he watched her scuttle down the cobblestone, he scanned the market. Within moments, he had his answer.

Joseph had walked over to a man he had dealt with occasionally in the past. One of the Zealots, the man would have no problem obeying orders from him.

He quickly whispered into the man's ear and the man left quickly, taking the same direction that Clandaugh had taken moments before. Within minutes, he was back. He handed Joseph the two small gold coins and received two larger ones in return. Joseph knew from the coins that the woman would bother him no more.

Later that day, he sent soldiers to the temple to look for Miriam. They found neither her nor the child she had been pregnant with when she left his home. He knew the High Priestess was hiding her, but felt he could do nothing more. Even using the soldiers had been a risk. He had explained to the chief of the Roman Guard that his grandchild had been kidnapped by one of the priestesses of the temple. Since neither the priestess or the child had been found, the matter had been dropped.

***

More than a year had passed and now he had more pressing things on his mind. What to do about Miriam was first and foremost. Yahshua was due back in days and he would not allow the two to meet. As he once more stood outside the heathen temple, he was surprised to hear a voice behind him.

"You could have her stoned, Father." His eldest son Barabbas said.

"How can I do that? Everyone would know then she is my daughter."

"Not necessarily, Father. I could have her dragged from the temple as a Jew breaking the law. Your name would never come into it."

"How could you do that? By what authority?"

"I'll have one of the priests to back me up. The girl will no longer be a problem for you."

"I would in no way be connected to the girl? You can guarantee this?"

"I can guarantee this, Father. Today."

"Then, so be it." Joseph answered. He watched Barabbas weave his way through the crowd toward the Holy Temple. The afternoon shadows were already lengthening in the market place. He found a darkened corner and sat down to wait.

***

The loss of Vivienne weighed heavy upon Miriam's heart. Although many months had passed, they had received no word yet about whether they had

55

arrived safely or not, Miriam could only hope for the best. To occupy her mind, she continued with her duties of teaching the neophytes and her new job of entertaining the guests of the temple. It was by doing this that Miriam felt she could pay Mircalla back for the coins lent to pay for Ariade and the child to reach Avalon.

Miriam could not stay busy enough as she tried hard not to think about her daughter, her homeland, or what she was doing. Yet she couldn't say she was unhappy, only lonesome. She had become close friends with Mircalla over this time. It was the High Priestess that had reminded her that Yahshua's three years were nearly over. She could only hope now that he would be able to find her. She was sure that her father would take delight in telling Yahshua how she was making her way in this strange land.

Chapter Eleven

Miriam had just left the last visitor of the evening when the doors of the temple slammed open revealing a man of the priesthood and the Roman Guard. As she and Mircalla stood amazed, as the Jewish man approached them. Two of the Romans grabbed Miriam while the others stood blocking Mircalla from intervening.

"This woman is a Jew and must face the punishment of our laws. Do not attempt to stop us or we will see to it that Pilot learns of your own deceits."

With that, they began to drag Miriam kicking and screaming from the temple. At the foot of the steps they handed her over to the priest and several other Jewish men. By her hair and arms, the men paraded her through the streets of Jerusalem. The pace slowed only when the party reached a large quarry pit.

Standing at the rim of the quarry, they pulled Miriam to her feet and forcefully pitched her into the pit.

In her fear, Miriam looked around. More than a dozen men stood lining the sides of the cavity she was in. As she looked from face to face, she was not surprised to see her father and Barabbas there as well.

"This woman is of Jewish heritage." A voice rang out and continued, "She has wantonly broken the laws of God by allowing her body to be used outside of marriage. If that is not enough, we have testimony that she gives her sexual favors to the Romans on the Sabbath. What say ye all, leaders of Israel?"

"Stone her!" The words rang in unison from them all.

The stones began hitting her body and within seconds, she crouched into a squatting fetal position in an attempt to shield her head and body from the flying rocks.

Then it stopped, as quickly as it had begun and Miriam felt strong arms reaching down to lift her up. She wiped her eyes in order to see the man who was her savior.

"Yahshua, you are here." Came her quiet reply.

"Yahshua, this has nothing to do with you. We are only carrying out the law." Miriam heard the words of her father. Other voices echoed the same sentiment.

Yahshua stooped and picked up two rocks and held them out in his hands.

"Let he among you that is without sin, cast the first stone." Saying this, he crouched down and picked up a stick. Into the dirt before him, he began writing the names of the men standing around the pit. Behind each name, he wrote the laws of God that each had broken.

One by one, the men left until only Joseph and Barabbas remained.

"Uncle, I have just returned from my mother's house. We are preparing a wedding."

"Whose wedding is that?" came the older man's reply. "What has that to do with her?"

"My mother is making the arrangements for my marriage, Uncle. My marriage to Miriam."

"You cannot do this, Yahshua."

"I can do this and you have no say in the matter, Uncle. By your very act here, you have disowned your own daughter. She is now a free woman to do as she wishes." Turning to Miriam, he asked, "You will still be my wife?"

"It is what I have waited for." She replied.

"Then it is settled, Uncle. We marry in Cana in a week's time. You alone can make the choice of whether you wish to join us there."

"I told you he would be a disappointment to you father." Both Miriam and Yahshua clearly heard Barabbas say as they walked away.

Chapter Twelve

Yahshua wrapped his arm around Miriam's shoulder. Tears were streaming down her face as he led her away from the pit.

"Do you know what I have done, Yahshua?" she asked.

"You have done what you needed to do, that is all."

"Yahshua..."

"Shush now, everything will be all right. I promised I would come back for you and I did. Let us go collect your belongings and start for Cana. We have a wedding to attend." He looked down at her and smiled.

She could only nod as she leaned her body against him. People in the street were staring, yet it seemed not to bother Yahshua. Without asking, he led her to the Temple. Turning her to face him, he looked deep into her eyes,

"I will linger here for you. Collect your belongings, say your good-byes. Take the time you need. It is my turn to wait for you."

Miriam's heart felt lighter than it had in years. She smiled back at him, once again feeling the love she had had since childhood.

"Go." he said, nodding toward the temple doors.

Miriam bounded up the stairs, determined to keep him waiting no longer than needed. Inside the temple the priestesses and neophytes gathered round her, wanting to know what happened. The constant buzz of chatter as she walked toward the living quarters ceased when Mircalla's voice cut through the din.

"Miriam, you are alive!" Mircalla's voice was shaky and as Miriam looked at her, she could tell the High Priestess had been crying.

"Yes, My Lady. Yahshua saved me."

"He has returned then?"

"Yes, My Lady, we are to be married in a week's time." Miriam said, suddenly shy.

"Then we are to lose you?"

"Yes..." Miriam replied, suddenly finding herself crying.

"Cry not, child. This is a happy occasion. Gather your things, I shall collect your dowry."

"My dowry?"

"No Priestess leaves this temple without blessings from Isis." Mircalla said smiling.

"But I owe you so much already."

"Your debt was paid a long time ago, Miriam. Now it is time for your happiness. Run along, I will meet you at the steps. I want to meet this man I have heard so much of."

With most of the priestesses following, Miriam finished making her way to the living quarters. She quickly bundled her few belongings and began the process of saying good-bye to the women who had been her only friends for the past three years. When hugs and tearful blessings had been said, she made her way back to the front of the Temple.

Mircalla stood waiting for her.

"I peeked outside. A very handsome man." She handed Miriam another bundle.

"What is all this? This is too much." Miriam said.

"It is your wedding dress. And a few other small trinkets." Mircalla answered with a smile.

Miriam could barely hold back the tears that threatened to fall from her eyes.

"Thank you Mircalla. You have been so kind to me; I will never forget the debt I owe you."

"You owe me nothing, child. Be happy that is all I ask. Now let us go meet this man of yours."

Mircalla pulled open the temple door and followed Miriam through and down the stairs to where Yahshua waited. Miriam made the necessary introductions.

"I thank you for taking care of the woman I love" Yahshua said looking Mircalla in the eye.

"She has been a dear friend to me, now I charge you with her care." the older Priestess' responded.

"I will not let you down, Priestess. I realize the treasure I have."

"Then I will hinder you no longer. Go in peace, with all the blessings of Isis."

"We thank you for your blessings, Lady. May you also always have peace."

Yahshua took the two parcels from Miriam gathering them under one arm. The other he placed protectively around her shoulder.

Miriam reached out for one last embrace with Mircalla.

"I shall miss you so." she said.

"And I you, child. Never forget who you are."

"I won't Mircalla."

"Go, now." The older woman said as she turned and returned to the Temple door.

Yahshua looked down at Miriam, "Are you ready, now?"

"I am ready." She replied, her face a mixture of smiles and tears.

***

Together they began the long journey to Cana. As they walked, they began talking about all that had happened in the last three years. Miriam listened as he spoke of his years with the Essene's and he held her attention completely as he described his forty-day sojourn in the desert, which was his final initiation into the society.

They walked four days before reaching the small town. The night before reaching the village, she told Yahshua everything that had happened to her while he was gone. As she told her story, fear gripped its fingers around her belly as she hoped that he would not hate her for the things she had done. When she got to the part about their daughter, she though the fear would break her, but she continued ahead until the conclusion.

"Do you still want me Yahshua, knowing what I have done?"

"You have done what you had to do. I knew it would not be easy for you. I knew you would have to make choices that you would hate. You did your best. And that is the end of it. We will never discuss it again."

Miriam almost collapsed from the relief she felt. She allowed him to hold her in his arms and allowed nature to follow its own course. Lying beside the fire, in the glow of their lovemaking, she asked about the wedding.

"Your mother, she will accept me?"

"She will. She knows the love I feel for you. She wants grandchildren. She wants a daughter."

"Will there be many people there? My father, do you think he will come?"

"It will be a small gathering. And no, I don't

think your father will make the journey. His secret is out now; it will be an embarrassment to him. I think Uncle Joseph will go back on another journey soon. He will leave Aunt Martha to his shame and the questions."

"Will he leave us alone, Yahshua?"

"Yes, I think he will now. In time, he may even come to accept our choices. Do not worry about him any longer. He can no longer hurt you."

Miriam curled into his shoulder, feeling safe. Her eyes heavy, she fell asleep and didn't move until he kissed her awake the following morning.

By midafternoon, they are arrived at Mary and Joseph's house in Cana. The compassion and friendliness of Yahshua's parents overwhelmed her. They greeted her as if they had known her forever.

Miriam sat alone at the table with Yahshua, his father Joseph, and his mother Mary. She could not resist the thought of how different this Joseph was compared to her own father. He had a quiet pleasant voice that sounded as if it had never known anger. His eyes were a deep brown that twinkled and seemed laughing at everything. Yahshua's mother, Mary, was a petite woman, yet full of grace. Smiling often, although surrounded by a very humble adobe house, the woman seemed not to have a care in the world outside of her husband and her son. As they ate, Mary finally asked the question that Miriam had been dreading,

"My son tells me I have a grandchild. Is she beautiful?"

"She is My Lady. Although barely two, she has the beauty of my mother and thankfully not of me." Miriam said with a smile.

"If we had only known your true plight, we would have come for you." Joseph interjected.

Overwhelmed with the kindness of these two

strangers, Miriam could only reply a soft,
"Thank you."

Mary spoke up, "My sister's husband is not always a good man. He does what he feels is right. No matter if that is true or not. His treatment of you was appalling."

"You are our daughter now." Joseph said.

No more was said during the rest of the meal. Miriam helped Mary clean after all were finished and the women talked about the upcoming wedding in two day's time.

Miriam tried to help with the preparations for the wedding, yet found most had already been taken care of before their arrival. The guests began arriving, so she busied herself finding space for extra pallets so all could sleep.

Chapter Thirteen

Joseph entered the small room where Judas was working the new leather.

"Son, I have a task for you to perform." he said.

Judas laid aside the camel hide he was scraping.

"Father, you know I will do as you ask." he replied.

"I ask that you go to Cana and stop this wedding. Neither I nor Barabbas will be allowed entry, but you were not a part of what happened at the quarry and I do not believe Yahshua will hold our actions against you."

"And how do you propose I stop the wedding, Father? Yahshua is a grown man and as he stated, you disowned Miriam, so you have no say over her either."

"Yahshua will listen to common sense, to reason. You of all people should know what it is like for outsiders in Judea. Make him see that he will only make Miriam's life a nightmare by marrying her. Convince him to send her back to the isle; they will both be happier in the long run."

"And Father, if I can't convince him, what then?"

His father glared at him, "If he will not listen to reason, do what you must. However, do not allow this wedding to occur. Do you understand, my son?"

Judas looked into his father's eyes and saw coldness in them he had never seen before.

"I understand, Father. When do I leave?"

"The servants are preparing your pack now. Everything should be at the ready in less than an hour."

"As you will, Father." Judas replied,

"This is the most important task I have ever asked you to perform. If you cannot accomplish this, do not return. This will no longer be your home."

Judas put away his tools. He found a stable hand and instructed him to finish the uncompleted hide. Going to his bedchamber, he packed a small satchel of personal belongings, his father's words echoing in his mind.

As his father promised, upon entering the stables, he found a donkey blanketed, along with two sacks of provisions. Mounting the donkey, he began the long trek to Cana.

The donkey trudged along the well-worn roadway and Judas allowed himself to think of the events of the last week.

He, like most people in his father's house, had wondered what had happened to Miriam when she disappeared. He had learned from a servant that his brother, Barabbas, had attempted to rape her the night she vanished. He, himself, had been awakened by the yelling and screaming being done by both Barabbas and his mother. His father had attempted to restore the calm only to find out that Miriam had fled the villa.

He knew inquiries had been sent out, but she had encountered no one on the streets of Jerusalem and therefore had slipped away undetected. Until this week, Judas had thought no one knew where she was. But listening to his father's angry conversation with Barabbas in the salon a few days earlier, he realized that the older man had known where Miriam was for quite a while.

Judas had been in the market when the Roman Guard and Caiaphas, the High Priest, stormed the Temple of Isis. Within minutes, Miriam was dragged outside by her hair. The guard had turned her over to other Jewish elders waiting below the temple steps. He had followed as they dragged her to the quarry.

He still hated himself for not trying to intervene. The girl was his sister; of that he was now almost sure. Miriam had done nothing but what she had been forced to do by the actions of his father and his brother. Yet, he had stood back and remained silent.

A prayer of thankfulness escaped from his lips as he saw Yahshua enter the pit. Very calmly, he had wrapped his arms around Miriam and with few words, the majority of the crowd dispersed. He had seen the anger on his father's face as Yahshua led Miriam away and back toward the temple.

Now his father wanted him to stop the marriage. He had even hinted murder if that was what it took and Judas knew he did not mean that for Yahshua. Had Joseph sent him on this journey to prove he was a man? Had he meant what he had said about not returning home if the wedding wasn't stopped? Could he give up his family and his home?

Judas knew that his father should have sent his brother Barabbas to do this job. Barabbas would have no problem fulfilling his father's wishes, no matter the cost. Judas knew also that Barabbas had no love for his cousin, Yahshua. He had ranted many times while drunken with wine of how Joseph had bestowed blessings on Yahshua that should have been his.

The further he progressed away from Jerusalem toward Cana, Judas knew that he would not follow that option, no matter the outcome of his talk with his cousin. As he made camp for the night, his heart felt lighter. If he couldn't talk his cousin out of this, then so be it; he would find a new life elsewhere. Far away from the hate of his brother Barabbas and the guilt of his father.

Entering the city gates of Cana the next morning, Judas led the donkey to his Aunt's home. Mary, his mother's sister, was a woman totally different from his mother. Mary had no ambitions for worldly possessions. She had shown Judas nothing but kindness and love since he had been a small child.

He stopped the donkey in front of the small house she shared with her carpenter husband, dismounted and walked up the pathway to the door.

Mary, herself, threw the door open upon his knock and showered him with hugs and kisses.

"Judas, my nephew, you have come for the wedding. I was afraid that side of the family had abandoned us altogether." She said, her eyes twinkling in the late afternoon sun.

"Aunt Mary, I could never abandon you." Judas exclaimed, "But I do need to talk to Yahshua. Is he here?"

"You've come to talk him out of it. I'm sure your father put you up to this." Mary said, her laughter now gone, a frown replacing the smile. "Yes, he is here. I will see if he will see you."

Mary turned and disappeared into a room off the main entry. She returned a few moments later and said,

"He said you can try. But that you'll be wasting your breath. Follow me."

She led him into the second room where Yahshua, Miriam and Joseph were quietly talking.

"We were about to have supper, I'll prepare an extra seat, you must be famished after your journey."

"You know why I have come?" Judas asked.

"I know." Yahshua replied, "I've been expecting you."

"Expecting me?"

"Who else would he send? He is desperate now.

I am no longer following his dictates and that's not the way he wants it."

"He's worried about your happiness. And hers." Judas said.

"Our happiness, no, my cousin, that is not what this is about at all. He has lost control over a situation that he felt he had total authority over. This is more about his own failure."

"I don't understand. What failure?" Judas asked.

"Do you really think your father invested so much time and money into me and my studies without expecting a return? A reward, per se?"

Judas sat down on the floor, "I had not really thought about it." he replied.

"Why would he do that for a poor nephew and not his own sons?" Yahshua asked.

Judas grew quiet; he had no answers to his cousin's questions, no more than he had answers to his own.

Mary returned carrying a platter laden with bowls and sat it on the floor between the two men. Miriam stood and left, returning with a large pitcher and wooden chalices.

"Talk later, eat now." Mary said as she passed a bowl to each man. Miriam filled the chalices and passed them also. They ate in silence, and Judas felt each of them watching him as he struggled with his own thoughts. When the meal was completed, Yahshua stood,

"Shall we go for a walk under the stars, cousin? We have much to discuss and the women still have a wedding to plan."

He leaned over and kissed Miriam on the forehead, "We shall return soon, my love."

Judas watched the two together and saw the love shared between them. He knew then, nothing he could say would stop this marriage from happening.

***

The two men walked in silence until they reached the outskirts of the village. Once on the dirt path leading away from the possibility of being overheard, Yahshua asked,

"You cannot do what you have been sent here to do, can you, my brother?"

Judas averted his eyes from Yahshua's face, "What is that?" he asked.

"Are you not here to stop this marriage?"

"I am, that was the task my father gave me."

"And how far are you willing to go to carry out your father's wishes?" Yahshua asked quietly.

Judas lifted his head to look his cousin in the eyes. "Not as far as he might wish."

"And the consequences for failing?"

"I will have no home, no family, no livelihood."

Yahshua laughed, "Am I not family, Judas?"

The younger man smiled, "You are, cousin."

"Then have no worries about family. Do you know why your heart told you that you cannot do what your father has asked?"

"Because I am not the man my brother Barabbas is. I cannot be so cruel."

"No, but you are everything your twin is. Kind, compassionate, loyal."

Yahshua watched as his words began to sink into Judas' thoughts.

"My twin? Miriam? How could that be?"

"You are born of the same mother, your birth was only moments before Miriam's. It is that bond that began in the womb that keeps you from harming her."

"How do you know this, Yahshua?"

"I was there. On the Isle as news of your birth came. Your father came and took you away, bringing you to Jerusalem."

"Does Miriam know?"

"She may suspect you are her brother, but I doubt if she knows for sure. Male children born on the Isle were often fostered out to other families and no male can live there after the age of five seasons. Either that, or the mother left the priesthood."

Judas smiled, "So males are undesirable as children." He shook his head, "Quite the opposite is true here."

Yahshua smiled. "I will ask you this favor, Judas. Do not reveal this to Miriam just yet."

"Why?"

"I want her to come to trust you first. You are from her father's house and right now, she doesn't know why you are here."

"But, I only plan to stay long enough for the wedding. Then I'll try to find my own way in the world. I cannot go back to my father's house."

"Stay with us, here. We will be leaving in due time. Truly get to know your sister and myself. I see a time in the future where I will have a need of you, both as a friend and ally. Will you do that?"

"I will do that, my cousin and brother. I will do whatever you ask, even to protecting you and my sister with my life."

"Hopefully, that won't be necessary." Yahshua laughed as he turned to the young man. "Shall we head back? I'm sure Miriam must think we are lost by now."

The two men turned on the path and began. heading back the way they had came

**

The morning of the wedding rose with a brilliant rising sun and clear skies.

"See a good omen." Mary said as she helped Miriam into the gown that Mircalla had given her. Made of pure silk, the soft, white gown with its light blue mantle was the most beautiful clothing Miriam had ever worn. The time arrived and she was seated on her wedding chair.

Yahshua was carried in on a liter by his younger brothers and childhood friends. The ceremony itself was short, with Yahshua's father speaking for the bride.

Vows were said, then the bride and groom settled in for the well wishes of the guests. Many had brought gifts for the couple. The wine began to flow and everyone seemed happy for them.

Miriam could not remember a day of such happiness. She found herself blushing like a virgin as the women carried her to her wedding bed. So much laughter, so much friendship, it made her feel as if she finally belonged somewhere. Not even on the Isle, had she felt such a feeling of kinship.

Only one person in the entire company of guests had said anything derogatory. A former visitor to the temple had objected to her being given a Jewish wedding. Yahshua and his father had both stepped up and told the man that it was not his concern, to worry more about where he stood in the eyes of his god instead of where she stood. The guest quickly left and the day went on without incident.

**

Two days later, many guests still remained. Miriam overheard Mary tell Yahshua they were almost out of wine. He pointed to three large urns and said they were full. Mary said they couldn't be, and Miriam had to agree as she had helped empty them, refilling them with water herself. But at Yahshua's insistence, the older woman went and looked.

Lifting the lid, and dipping a scoop, she had brought it to her lips, tasting. The ladle fell from her hands as she stared at her son. Miriam rushed to her side. The water was indeed wine. Miriam looked at her husband, wondering what magic he held. She had seen the druid priests perform magic, but nothing like this.

Collecting herself, she helped Mary fill the wine jugs that the servers brought to them. While still not understanding the mystery, Miriam was not going to let it touch her happiness.

Miriam overheard Yahshua and his father talking a week later.

***

"The man that insulted you at the wedding is a Zealot. I've been hearing talk in the village. It is not safe here for you or for your bride."

"I know who he was, Father. We have nothing to fear from him or the other Zealots. Uncle Joseph will keep Barabbas in line."

"What does Barabbas, have to do with this?"

"He is their leader, now at the present. Since the Roman's crucified the former. Uncle Joseph will keep him in line for no other reason than not to offend the Romans. They have been tolerant with my uncle."

"Do you think Joseph can do this?"

"He will have no choice, if he wishes to continue with the freedoms he has."

"I still worry, what if..."

"We, Miriam and I, will begin our journeys after the Sabbath. Moving targets are hard to catch." Yahshua responded, a smile upon his lips.

A look of worry crossed Miriam's face. Had there been death threats, she wondered. What did her father have to do with the Zealots? Even in the Temple of Isis, the priestesses had been warned to avoid any contact with the radical Jewish group. And what journey? Yahshua had not mentioned that to her. Miriam walked back toward the house, as she walked she wondered how many other things were being kept from her. Mary might know, she thought and became determined to ask.

She found her mother in law grinding flour for the evening bread. Picking up a rock, Miriam pulled another stone bowl toward her and filled it with dry wheat kernels. As she ground the tiny grains into flour, she asked,

"Have you heard the rumor of the Zealots?"

Mary looked up from her work. "I have daughter, I too am worried."

"Yahshua seemed to think nothing of it."

"Yahshua has been gone these three years; he does not yet understand how strong they have become."

"Do you think we are safe?" Miriam asked.

"As safe as possible in these days. Your father will protect the both of you, even if he would prefer not to."

"Why would he do that?" Miriam asked.

"Your father has put all his hope into your husband. Nothing will deter him from the future he has planned."

"He has planned Yahshua's future?"

"Every detail. But that is all I can say. The rest is best to come from your husband."

Miriam continued to grind wheat, yet paid little attention to what she was doing. As the day wore on, she helped Mary with all that she could to have her new family's meal prepared when the men returned. Her mind, lost in thought and concern, was unable to help her think through all that she had overheard and been told. Finally, shaking her head, she realized she would have to wait until Yahshua was ready to tell her exactly what was happening.

Chapter Fourteen

The heat of the summer sun felt intense on Miriam's skin. Hidden as she was in men's clothing, she did not have the comfort of the lighter linen fabrics both the Roman and Jewish women wore at the height of summer. A soft breeze blowing off the Sea of Galilee helped some to cool her face, yet could not penetrate the layers of garments that she wore.

Yahshua had been preaching the goodness of God's love for the Jewish nation for months now. Going from village to village, encampment to encampment, laying their heads anywhere that would offer them rest for the evening. Many nights had been spent lying in the open on sandy and graveled ground. What had started as only herself and Yahshua, now stood as a band of over twenty. The gospel her husband was teaching had made converts along the way. Many sacrificing home and family to follow their new master.

Miriam placed her hand upon her belly. Her time was near, she thought, as she felt the child moving. Another week or two and she would again hold a child in her arms and at her breast.

Her mother in law was with them now, as her husband, Joseph, had died two months before. His death, spoken of in only whispers and secrecy, had come at the hands of the Zealots. The father of Yahshua had refused to tell them of his son's plans. In return, an assassin had slid a knife into his ribs in the marketplace of Cana, leaving him to die in the mud and filth of the streets.

Mary alone had traveled to find her son and bring him the news of his father, Joseph's death.

Yahshua had tried to convince his mother to

return to her home of Nazareth, but the older woman refused, preferring to stay with her son and daughter in law; claiming them as the only family she had remaining. In the days following Mary`s arrival, the decision to disguise Miriam was made. Yahshua had explained that it was for her safety as so many newcomers were traveling with the band. His mother would carry the child on their journeys after the birth, and most would assume that it was a late pregnancy. The child would have to feed in secrecy until things felt safe once more. Yahshua had even renamed her, calling her Magdalene; his tower of strength. Only those few that had traveled with them since the beginning knew the truth and were sworn to secrecy. Now she, to all outward appearances, was just another male follower.

Yet, Miriam had to smile at the rare moments that Yahshua planned and worked out for them to be alone together. In those times, she was allowed to be the woman and wife she was. She treasured every simple pleasure; as she always felt a measure of fear in their day-to-day life. She too, had heard the rumors and the grumblings of the hecklers, the unconvinced and the zealots.

No matter her husband's reassurances, Miriam knew that their lives were always in danger. And yet they went on.

Leaving the Sea of Galilee, they had three new followers. Peter, John and his brother James. Miriam had taken an instant dislike to Peter, seeing him as power hungry, willing to do anything to have the adoration that John and James showed Yahshua. Yet, her husband seemed blind to this, appearing to draw closer to Peter than the others.

When questioned, Yahshua had only told her

that yes, he was aware of Peter's nature, but that it was all part of the way it should be. She could never get him to discuss the 'what' of the 'should be'.

The next stop on their journey was to be Nazareth, Yahshua's boyhood home. It was there that she hoped to give birth. Yahshua had promised that they would rest there for many days before making the trip to Jerusalem. She dreaded that trip as she had few good memories. Yahshua had told her that she could revisit her friends at the temple if she desired and could hide herself there during the sojourn in the city.

***

Judas listened carefully from his hiding place among the overhanging rocks, as his brother spoke to the small band of Zealots. Already the group had tried three times to kill either Yahshua or one of his followers. Now they were again plotting the death of his cousin. The sun above the rocky terrace was beating into his back, yet he knew one movement, one sound would give his location away. Brother or not, Judas knew that Barabbas would have no qualms in killing him, so he endured the blistering sun and listened to his brother's plans.

"We have tried assassination, we have tried mercenaries, this has not worked, my brothers." Barabbas's voice was full of venom. "Yet, I think I know a way to rid us of this menace."

"How? As you say, we have tried and failed. Maybe it is the will of God that he lives." One of the men said, making it sound more a statement of fact than a question.

Judas watched as his brother swirled around to face the questioner. "Surely you do not believe that,

Abram?"

"I do not know what to believe any longer, Barabbas. They say he heals the sick, restores sight to the blind, and mends the lame. And that is only the beginning of the miracles people say about him."

Judas could feel the coldness in his brother's eyes as he glared at the man. "We do not have room for doubts. Either you believe me that this man is a danger to us all or you are free to go join the miracle worker yourself."

The two men stared at each other for a long moment before Abram spoke, "Then I will go." Abram stepped back, picked up his satchel, and turned to walk away. Judas watched as his brother withdrew his dagger from his sleeve and threw it into the man's back. Abram fell to the sand without taking a second step.

"Anyone else wish to leave?" Barabbas asked.

The remaining men all shook their heads no.

"Then this is what we must do. My spy has told me that Yahshua and his followers will be in Jerusalem for Passover. That is in six days. During his stay, we will tarnish his image with the people and we will enflame the Sanhedrin to the point where they want him dead."

"How do we do that?" a deep voice asked.

"You will all do your part. For everyone he heals, make them die. Myself, I will pose as him and disrupt the temple. For six years, all I have heard is that I am him in his looks. Now, I will use that to my advantage."

"Do you not fear that God will punish you Himself if you do this thing, Barabbas?" The same voice asked.

"Our cause is just and righteous. God will reward us all. We have much to plan, come, let us find shade from this sun."

Judas watched as each man picked up his pouch and followed Barabbas back toward the city. When he knew he could no longer be observed, he stood and brushed the sand from his clothing and began the journey back to Nazareth where Yahshua and his followers were waiting for his report.

As he walked, he wondered how he would counteract his brother's plan. Judas knew full well that Barabbas was right, if he caused upset in the temple, he would surely die. His brother was also correct in that he looked enough like Yahshua to pass for him easily. If Barabbas were careful and cunning, everyone in attendance would believe it was indeed his cousin.

Judas also knew his brother had enough friends within the Sanhedrin that would support his actions. Many in the Jewish priesthood feared the message Yahshua was bringing to the people, they feared his pull over the people. Both the Pharisees and the Sadducees saw Yahshua as a threat to an ageless way of life.

Stopping only to sleep for a few hours, by the time Judas entered Nazareth, he had a plan of his own. He might not be able to stop the arrest of Yahshua if Barabbas saw his plan though, but he did know how to keep him off a Roman pike pole

As he approached, the house the group was staying in, all he had left to figure out was how to get Yahshua to go along with it. Judas wiped his brow and removed his sandals before entering the house. He would have to enlist some help from among the followers, but wondered whom he could trust. With a few moments of thought, he knew; James and John. Peter would have to be kept in the dark; the one thing Judas shared with Magdalene was her absolute distrust of Peter the fisherman.

.

Chapter Fifteen

Miriam felt the first labor pangs just as they reached the gates of Nazareth. As the troop continued to walk through the city streets, the pain in her belly became almost unbearable. Mary, sensing her discomfort, spoke to Yahshua about finding a place of rest soon. Miriam could only offer a weak smile when Yahshua turned and looked at her with concern.

Mary came back to Miriam's side and began leading her toward a small house away from the crowds gathered around Yahshua. As they approached the doorway, an elderly woman stepped outside. Her skin, wrinkled and leathered from too many years in the sun, smiled.

"Mary, my daughter. It has been many years." The old woman's eyes lit up as she recognized the older woman.

"Mother, it is good to see you also. I am afraid I am going to have to ask your hospitality once more." Mary replied.

"My house is always your house. Anything I have is yours." came the response.

"My daughter-in-law is about to give birth. Do you have a pallet she may lie on?"

The elderly woman came to Miriam's side. "Of course, of course." Taking Miriam's arm, the two women supported her as they led her inside.

"I hoped I would someday meet my granddaughter. I had no way to travel the journey to the wedding. It will be good to witness the birth of my great grandchild."

Once inside, the elderly woman wasted no time getting a bed ready for the birth. Once Miriam was reclining, Mary and the older woman began gathering the supplies that would be needed. Miriam removed the turban from her head and allowed her long hair to flow down her back. She folded the turban into a pillow and began removing her outer clothing to make the birth easier. The contractions were coming steadily now, and Miriam knew she had merely minutes more before she would be holding her child.

From inside her small pack, she pulled a soft blanket and clean rags she had been collecting. The rags she placed in a bundle on the floor beneath her.

"Mary, I think it is time," she called out. The two women came to her side. The older woman supported her back as Mary lifted the undergarments from around her legs. As Miriam scrambled into a squatting position over the rags, she felt her child's head begin to push through.

Breathing heavily between the contractions, she tried to focus on the breath rather than the pain. As each contraction began, she allowed her body to push.

"The head is out, child. With the next push, the shoulders should be visible." Mary said quietly.

Another push and Mary said, "You have a son."

Although exhausted, Miriam could only smile. Leaning back on the older woman, Sarah, she waited for the afterbirth to expel and watched as Mary cleaned the body of the small child before her. Using two lengths of twine, Mary tied off the cord, cut between the two ties, wrapped the now squalling infant in the soft blanket, and laid the baby to the side of the pallet.

Using both hands, she pressed on Miriam's abdomen and Miriam felt the afterbirth slide from her body. Sarah helped Miriam to lie back on the pallet beside her newborn son.

"You did well, my daughter." Mary said with a

laugh as she began cleaning up the soiled rags. Sarah laid clean rags beneath Miriam's body and smiled.

"I have never, in my years, seen a woman go through that experience with such grace. Was there no pain at all?" she asked.

Miriam smiled weakly. "There was much pain, but I was trained in methods that allow you to limit the perception."

The elderly lady laughed, "You should teach that to Jewish women."

Now comfortable, Miriam picked up her newborn child and baring a breast allowed the child to nurse. He found the nipple quickly and began suckling.

"This one is a fast learner." She said looking at the two women. "I do not even know yet what Yahshua wishes to name him."

Mary turned from what she was doing in surprise, "You have not discussed a name?"

Miriam laughed. "We see so little of each other alone, that I supposed we've never talked about it for some reason."

She saw Mary smile, "As it should be, daughter. I'm sure he will be here as soon as he can. He will want to know about you and the child." Mary turned to Sarah, "Can I impose on you just a bit more?"

"Anything."

"I need to go tell my son about the birth. Will you watch over Miriam until my return? It should not be long."

"Go. Tell your son he is a father. They will both be safe here."

Miriam wondered how the older woman knew about the safety concerns, but the old woman was quick to address the issue.

"Word travels fast between cities. I know the

risks that my grandson faces and I know the risks that you face also. Yahshua is walking a path that is dangerous in these unsettled times. Between the Romans and the Zealots trying to bring about rebellion, words of peace have little value. And the Zealots will attempt to silence anyone who speaks them."

"You are wise Grandmother." Miriam said as she looked down at her now sleeping son.

"You should stay here while Yahshua goes to Jerusalem. It is the only safe place for both you and your child."

"I will consider these things, Grandmother and I thank you for your offer."

"You have time. I will talk to my grandson also. He should not place you and the child in danger. But for now, lay back and rest. The child will awaken you soon enough."

Miriam nodded and lay back on the pallet, placing the child in the safety of the crook of her arm. "Thank you, Grandmother." she said softly as her eyes closed.

When Miriam next opened her eyes, her husband was seated beside her.

"He is beautiful." Yahshua said. "May I hold him?"

Miriam lifted herself into a sitting position and handed him the infant.

"Joseph, I think, after my father." his eyes held a question.

"That is my father also." she replied.

"Then let us go with the older version, Joshua. That should satisfy."

"Joshua is good."

Miriam wanted to allow Yahshua to name the child since he had not attended Vivienne's birth and had no input on her name. Joshua was still an homage to his father and yet would not recall memories of how mistreated she had been by her own. As the infant began to squirm in his arms, he handed him back to Miriam.

"He has an appetite, I think. You have given me a strong son, my wife. I am humbled before you."

"Well, it took both of us to do it." She said laughing as she positioned the child to nurse. Looking back at her husband, she again saw seriousness in his eyes.

"We begin the journey to Jerusalem tomorrow," he said.

"But why?" She asked, "Passover isn't for weeks and I thought we were going to rest here for a while?"

Yahshua laughed a feeble laugh. "The people of Nazareth do not want me, nor do they wish to hear what I have to say. We have already moved outside the city gates and will camp there for the night."

"I will be ready by dawn." Miriam said.

"I have talked with both Mother and Grandmother. I wish for you, and my child, to stay here. You know of the Zealot's plans, I will be back for you as soon as Passover is complete. It will give you time to regain your strength."

"Yahshua, I ..."

"No arguments. My mind is made up. Should something happen, I will send for you, otherwise, stay here and be safe. Do this for me, Miriam."

"Will you stay here tonight, with us?" She asked, looking first at her newborn son and then at her husband.

"I will stay as long as I can." he replied, reaching out to stroke a tear from her wet cheek.

"I will do as you ask." She said quietly as the tears spilled down from her eyes.

Hours later, he picked up his canvas satchel and kissed her softly on the cheek.

"I will be back for you Miriam," he said, "I came for you last time and I will again."

Miriam could only nod as words of goodbye escaped her. Burying her head into his shoulder, she clung to him as long as possible. Finally, he pulled away.

"I must go now. Be strong, take care of my son and I will see you soon."

"Promise me, you will be careful in Jerusalem."

"I promise." He replied and then kissing her quickly was gone. She heard him outside saying goodbye to his mother and grandmother, and several moments later, they returned to the house.

"It was the right decision, Miriam. John will bring word of what is happening in Jerusalem every few days. That way, your fears can be alleviated."

"John will do that?"

"I asked my son for this and he agreed. John or James will come every few days."

"Thank you, Mother. You have lightened my heart."

"Have you named the child?" Sarah asked.

"His name is Joshua. Yahshua said it was an older form of Joseph."

"It is indeed, child. It is a strong name, a good name for a strong son. This son will bring blessings upon the world. You wait and see."

Miriam smiled as she lay back on the pallet.

"You are tired. Rest while the child does."

Miriam nodded and turned to her side. Pulling the child close to her body, she allowed silent tears to lull her to sleep.

Chapter Sixteen

Yahshua was true to his word and every two or three days, John or James, in turn would arrive with word of the happenings in Jerusalem before heading back to the capital. The news at first was very good, as each of the men told of Yahshua's welcome when he returned to the city. Even her own father had given them a welcome feast.

As the week before Passover approched, Miriam could sense that neither John nor James was telling her everything. While they attempted to make it sound as if all was going well, there was apprehension in their voices. Finally, she felt she had to ask.

"You must tell me the truth, John. What is happening in Jerusalem?"

"There is much discord, Miriam. Yahshua said we wouldn't be able to keep it from you and he was right. Sometimes I think you see right through me."

"Tell me, John, what is happening."

"Judas was right. Barabbas is stirring up trouble and in some big ways. He is allowing himself to be identified as Yahshua and is angering both the priests with his words as well as the Romans. Judas is trying to discredit Barabbas, as is your father, but no one in authority wants to listen."

"So why does Yahshua stay? Can you not talk him into leaving that city?" Miriam could hear the fear in her voice.

"We have tried Miriam, we have tried. He says he will leave after the Passover dinner and not before."

"I pray that will be soon enough." she said

"We all pray it will be soon enough." John said, shaking his head, "We just don't know what Barabbas

90

will do next."

After John left to return to Jerusalem, Miriam fretted as she helped around Sarah's home and cared for her son. She checked out the doorway frequently in hopes to see James' arrival with news. No news came.

After two days, Miriam could stand it no longer.

"I'm leaving for Jerusalem tomorrow." she said, "There is something terrible happening there, I know. Yahshua is in trouble and I fear greatly for him."

"You cannot take the child into danger." Sarah said in reply.

"I will have too. I fear if I do not go, I will never see my husband again. I must do this."

The two other women exchanged glances.

"Then I shall go with you." Mary replied, "I have no choice as I cannot let you go alone on the roads. There is danger enough for a woman travelling alone."

At dawn the next morning, Miriam kissed Sarah goodbye. The old woman had tears in her eyes as she held the child one last time.

"I thank you Grandmother for all that you have done for me, a stranger. Your kindnesses will be repaid, of that I am sure." Miriam said as she took the child and placed it in the sling around her body.

"Miriam, I have come to love you as my own. No matter what happens, you will always be welcome here. This too is your home now."

Tears formed in Miriam's eyes as she nodded and uttered another thank you. She watched as her mother in law and the older woman said their goodbyes and then the two women were on their way, following the road to Jerusalem.

"If we're lucky, and God's willing, maybe we'll meet them on the road." Mary said as they walked.

"God and Goddess willing, I too wish they would make it so."

***

Things had gone worse than Judas feared since their arrival in Jerusalem. While the crowds greeted Yahshua enthusiastically, one look at either the priests or Roman soldiers told him that the tension in the city was running high.

Judas had already received many reports of things that Yahshua had done here or done there that were impossible. But for those who didn't know Yahshua, the actions of Barabbas were easy to blame on an almost twin. Tonight Passover would begin and within two days, if their luck held out, they could be away from the city. For now, it was time for them to go to the temple to pay the obligatory tithe. While there, he hoped to talk to Caiaphas and explain to the High Priest that it was his brother, not Yahshua that was causing the trouble in the city.

Weaving through the throngs of people who filled the streets of Jerusalem, Judas attempted to keep the masses away from Yahshua. Rumors abounded in the city that Yahshua had the ability to heal the sick, drive out demons and other miracles and supernatural happenings. Judas knew all of this to be untrue. Yahshua offered people only hope, and a faith in love that was far greater than themselves. Yet the rumors followed them everywhere.

While some of Yahshua's teachings were radical, they were neither heretical nor blasphemous. This is what he hoped to convince Caiaphas while at the temple. He would use his father's good standing to gain an audience. For now though, protecting Yahshua from Barabbas was his first concern.

They heard the commotion inside the temple before they climbed the stairs leading to the main doors. Once inside, Judas was astounded at what he saw.

Barabbas was running wildly from one vendor table to another, toppling them, spilling money everywhere. The entire temple was in chaos. Like Yahshua, Barabbas had a group of men with him doing the same. Moments later, Caiaphas entered the main temple and began yelling.

"What is the meaning of this?"

Barabbas paused in his rampage and glared at Caiaphas.

"You have turned my father's house into a den of thieves."

"Your father? Who are you who blasphemes so?" Caiaphas' voice boomed across the now quiet temple.

"Who am I?" Barabbas began, "I am Yahshua, the son of God."

Judas turned to Yahshua, "You must leave now, my Master. Before it is too late. Go!"

He then turned to John and James, "Get him out of here; it is not safe any longer."

Caiaphas screamed across the temple, "Capture that man," pointing to Barabbas.

"Go now!" Judas yelled to Yahshua, "Go now!"

He watched as John, James and the rest of the party led Yahshua back down the temple steps and toward the inn where they were staying. Only Peter had remained to watch the ensuing chaos as both roman guards and young priests attempted to capture

Barabbas. Judas turned back to the outrage in the temple only to find that Barabbas had disappeared, along with many of his followers. Several men were being held by the vendors, but Barabbas was not one of them. He had escaped.

Judas turned to Peter, "You did not go to protect the Master, why?"

"I wanted to watch what happened here. Who was that man who looks so like Yahshua?" Peter asked.

"The man is Barabbas, he wishes our Master dead."

"And you know this, how?"

"I know this, because I know Barabbas well. He is my brother. I know fully what he is capable of." Judas replied.

"What threat is Yahshua to him?" Peter asked his voice skeptical.

"Barabbas is a zealot, he wants war with Rome. Our Master's teachings do not advocate war. He is afraid people will listen."

"No one told me Yahshua had enemies. How long have you known? Why have you kept this secret from the rest of us?"

Judas could feel his temper rising. "I owe you nothing. I only owe my allegiance to the Master. He knows. Now get away from me, I have business to attend."

"Business with whom?" Peter persisted.

"That is nothing to you." Judas retorted and crossed the temple in search of Caiaphas.

Order was slowly being restored in the temple. A few moneychangers were arguing among themselves over which scattered money was theirs, but otherwise things had settled down quickly once the presence of the Roman guards began patrolling the floor.

Judas found the High Priest in a far corner of the main temple behind a pillar.

"Caiaphas, I need to have a conversation with you. Privately." Judas said.

"And you are?" Came the disinterested reply.

"Judas, son of Joseph of Arimathea."

"I will see you, if only for your father's sake. Follow me."

Judas followed the High Priest into a small anti-chamber.

"So?" Caiaphas asked.

"That man out there was not Yahshua. That was Barabbas, my brother."

"Why would he lie?"

"You know as well as I, that Barabbas is now leader of the Zealots. He would gain much by destroying the message of love preached by my Master, Yahshua."

"They say Yahshua can perform miracles. Is this true?"

"No rabbi, it is not. It is rumor and lies. My Master preaches nothing more than the grace of god, nothing else."

"I would like to meet this man. Can you arrange it for me?"

"I can, rabbi. After the Passover meal, we have plans to meet in the Garden of Gethsemane after dark fall. My Master likes to go there to pray."

"Then I will meet you there." Caiaphas replied, "Now I must be about my duties."

Judas knew he was dismissed. Leaving the temple, he hoped this meeting would prove to the priesthood that they had nothing to fear from Yahshua. He hurried back to the Inn.

As he made his way, he wondered what exactly Barabbas' motives truly were. He knew his brother had been jealous of his cousin since boyhood, but he didn't know when that jealousy had turned into such hatred. He did not understand his brother's actions and decided to go talk to his father.

He turned away from the Inn and began the walk to his father's villa. With his mind filled with thoughts, he paid little attention to the people on the streets, until someone grabbed his arm. He turned around only to find Yahshua's mother standing behind him.

"Mary, why are you here? We left you safe, in Nazareth."

"I am here because Miriam would not stay. She fears for Yahshua and feels she must be at this side. Will you tell me where my son is staying?"

Judas looked around, but didn't see Miriam anywhere.

"Where is Miriam now?" he asked.

"She has taken the child to the Temple of Isis. She knows he will be safe there."

Judas ran his fingers through his hair, worry filling his face. He had not planned on this complication. It was hard enough to protect Yahshua, now he would have to protect his wife and mother.

"Mary, you need to convince her to go back to Nazareth. It is not safe here in this city and I cannot watch out for all of you."

"She will not leave and I will not leave her alone." Mary replied.

"I will not leave. Please take me to my husband, Judas." Miriam's voice sounded from behind him. He turned and saw determination on the young woman's face. Resigned, he said,

"Come, I'll take you to him."

Nothing more was said as Judas led them back to the Inn. At the doorway before entering, he whispered to Miriam, "Watch out for Peter, I do not trust him."

"Nor do I, Judas. Nor do I."

"Tell my Master I will return shortly, before dark fall. I need to speak with our father first."

"I will tell him, Judas."

Judas nodded and turned. He only had a few hours before dusk and his business with his father must be completed before then. He would not be able to travel back to the Inn once the Passover holy day had begun. He quickly retraced his steps back in the direction of his father's villa.

Chapter Seventeen

The courtyard of the villa was filled with activity as he entered. No one stopped his progress into the house and he found his father alone in the salon, drinking a chalice of wine.

"Father, what hand does yours have in what Barabbas is doing?"

Judas was met by a stony stare from his father.

"I know Barabbas would do nothing that is against your will. You could put a stop to these lies and impersonations of his with just a word. Why have you not?"

"It is not part of the plan, my son. Everything that is happening is according to prophecy, it must happen for the prophecy to be fulfilled."

"What prophecy, Father?"

"The return of the Messiah. Only Yahshua has the bloodline to satisfy the requirements. Only if he becomes the Messiah will our people revolt against Rome and become free once more."

"Yahshua has no desire to be the next Messiah. Does he have no say in this matter?"

"He has none. He is my nephew; I have raised him and educated him. He will repay me by following the plan to the end."

"And what is the end, Father? Do you plan to have him die? Because if not, you had best stop Barabbas, for that is what he is trying to accomplish."

"It will not go that far, I will see to it."

"And if you cannot?"

"Then what happens, happens."

"I will protect Yahshua, Father."

"So you say, but you will not harm your own brother. Of that I am sure."

"Don't be so sure. Barabbas is dangerous to us all and I will protect Yahshua and my sister from both of you."

"So the little tramp is still with him?" Judas could hear the venom in his father's voice.

"Miriam is not a tramp, she is my Master's wife. And she is still your daughter."

"I disowned her years ago, just as I should have done to you."

Judas caught his breath. "I thought you already had, father. I will remove myself from your life on my own."

With those words, Judas turned and stormed from the salon. Rage filled him. Yahshua had told him that Miriam was his blood sister, but now he knew it for sure. He had never met a woman like her before; strong, determined and willful. He was proud to call her family. He walked back to the Inn knowing for certain that one of the mysteries of his life had now been solved.

Joining the others in the room, he told Yahshua of his meeting with Caiaphas.

"Once he meets you, he will know it was not you in the temple today."

Judas saw a worried look in Yahshua's eyes,

"It may be too late. The Roman guards are looking for this Yahshua everywhere. I do not think I'll fare well with the Roman's do you?"

"We'll work it out, Master. This I promise."

"It will work out to God's will, Judas. It is no longer left up to man."

Judas felt the rage returning as Yahshua placed an arm around his shoulder. How could his Master be so unconcerned about his fate?

"Many things are a mystery, Judas, many things. At least you now have confirmation of all I told you."

"How...?"

"It doesn't matter how I know. I do ask a promise of you though."

"Anything Master."

"No matter what happens, promise you will watch out for Miriam, my child and my mother. Do I have your vow on this?"

"I will give my life to protect them from harm, Master. You have my word."

"Then, let no more be said. Come, let us join the others."

Judas allowed Yahshua to lead him back to where the others were congregated. As usual, Yahshua began telling stories; stories of farmers and stories of black sheep.

Judas found he couldn't listen. His mind raced. As he looked at the faces of those around the room, he wondered if all were devoted enough to the Master not to turn him in to the Roman guard. His eyes fell on Miriam. Of all the people in this room, besides Yahshua, she was the only person he trusted without question. Her and Mary, only two women were devoted enough in his eyes to stand beside Yahshua no matter the circumstances.

Tomorrow night, Judas hoped to convince Caiaphas to talk with Pilot and recall the warrant for Yahshua's arrest. Then they could leave this city and Barabbas could do them no more harm. Yet Judas knew now, not only was he fighting his brother, but was now fighting his father as well. He only could hope that he would win this battle. The new Messiah, indeed. How could his father believe that he could force prophecy to be fulfilled?

Judas reached for the pitcher of wine in the center of the room. Taking his cup from his belt, he filled it and drank the cup quickly. Refilling the cup, he prayed that they could get away from all of this without further incident.

Chapter Eighteen

Miriam stayed quiet throughout the meal, although the conversation flowed between the other twelve men and Yahshua. Peter began pressing the cause of fighting for freedom against the Romans, while James and John both asserted the time for rebellion had not yet arrived.

"Why not?" Peter demanded. "Look at the following Yahshua has. He could raise an army twenty thousand strong in days. It would only take one battle to double our strength."

"So now you wish to lead a rebellion, Peter?" Judas asked as he began paying more attention to the conversation. "Has that ever been part of the Master's plan? I did not realize you were a zealot also."

Miriam watched as Peter slammed his wine cup onto the table.

"I am no zealot!" Peter replied. "I just see an opportunity. We are strong; we are growing in number daily. We are all sick of this occupation. Yahshua has the power to bring together the people."

"Go back to your fishing, Peter. As the others have said, now is not the time."

"There's never going to be the time, at least not in your mind, is there Judas?"

"The time will come when we are all free." Judas answered, "But now, it is dangerous times we live in and Yahshua is not safe in this city."

"It is too bad you do not have the courage of your brother, Judas. He is not afraid of Rome."

"My brother is a fool, as are you."

Miriam saw Peter's fists clench and was afraid the two men would come to blows over the issue.

Looking at Judas, she saw he had gone back to his wine and was talking quietly with John. Peter's face continued to show rage and Miriam, at that moment, realized how dangerous this man could be.

Not that he would do anything outwardly, she thought. No, Peter was the type who would stab a man in the back if it justified his own means. Perhaps she should warn Judas. She thought about it for a moment or two and decided that no, Judas was smart enough to know who his enemies were. Yet she would continue to watch Peter herself.

Her attention was captured by Nathaniel, who sat next to her at the table, when he asked Yahshua,

"Master, with the guard looking for you, how will we escape the city?"

"We will leave in small groups, no more than two or three men at a time. We can all meet together again in Damascus in a few weeks."

"Are you sure you will be safe, Master?" Nathaniel asked.

"I'll have Judas, John and James to protect me if needed."

Miriam watched her husband's face as he said those words and saw the worry in his eyes. Her intuition told her that he knew that something terrible was about to happen and that is why he was sending the others so far away. She felt knots form in her stomach and wished she could talk to her husband alone, but knew there was no way that could be arranged until after he had said his evening prayers.

She closed her eyes and said a quick prayer of her own to the goddess asking for protection for her husband. Her thoughts were interrupted by the raised voices of Judas and Peter. This time, they were loud enough that the entire room could hear their argument.

"You would let the Master die to serve your ends, would you not, Peter?"

"He would not die, I'm sure you would protect him, Judas. After all, we all know you would never betray him."

Miriam could hear sarcasm in Peter's voice and wondered why it was there.

"No, I never would betray him." Judas responded, "But you would deny him, by going against his teachings."

Yahshua slammed his fist on the table. "Enough."

The room went quiet.

"I am not here to begin a war, Peter. That is not my purpose. Have you listened to nothing I have said, Peter? The kingdom I promise you is not here on earth. It is in Our Father's house. What happens in this world is no concern of mine."

Miriam watched as Peter stared brazenly at Yahshua for a few moments before he sat down. Her husband continued to talk,

"There are those here tonight that will both deny me and betray me. It is the way of the world and what happens must happen. There is no other way, it is God's plan and will play out the way he wills. So let us stop arguing among ourselves and enjoy this meal together. It may well be our last."

Yahshua lifted his wine glass, "Let us all drink together as brothers." He took a sip of the wine and handed the cup to Nathaniel. The cup was passed from man to man, each taking a sip and handing it on to the next.

For the remainder of the meal, the conversations around the table were quiet and relaxed. Miriam would glance every now and again at Peter and Judas only to

104

see neither man was saying anything to anyone. Both were holding their tongues, not wanting to upset Yahshua any further.

When all the food had been consumed, Miriam and Mary began clearing the empty plates and bowls from the table.

"I worry for my husband." Miriam said in hush whispers to her mother in law.

"I fear for my son, also." Mary replied, "But it is man's work he is about and women have very little say in how a man handles his affairs."

Miriam could only nod at this statement and wish in her heart it wasn't so.

The room began to clear out as many of Yahshua's followers came up to him to say goodbye. Kissing their Master, each man promised to meet him in Damascus before the next full moon. They too were ready to leave Jerusalem, Miriam sensed, and feared for their own lives.

Soon all that remained in the room were Yahshua, Peter, John, James and Judas. Yahshua rose from the table and came to Miriam's side. He pulled her close.

"I go to pray now. Remember me." He kissed her lightly on the forehead. "No matter what happens, Miriam, know this; I love you."

"Something terrible is going to happen, isn't it?" she asked, holding back sobs.

"I do not know. Time alone will tell. Now, I must go." he said, breaking their embrace. "If I do not return tonight, listen to Judas and do what he tells you. Promise me this?"

Miriam looked into the eyes of the only man she had ever loved. "I will. I love you."

She closed her eyes and took a deep breath to

fight back the tears that were threatening to fall from her eyes.

"I will always love you, Miriam. Always, even in death." Yahshua said quietly before he turned and signaled to the others and left the chambers.

Miriam turned to her mother in law, "Oh Mary, what are we to do?"

Mary wrapped her arms around Miriam, holding her as she sobbed.

"All we can do, daughter, is pray. Pray and hope God will answer."

Chapter Nineteen

Judas was confident when they entered the Garden of Gethsemane that before the evening was over, one threat to Yahshua would be alleviated. Caiaphas would see that Yahshua was not attempting to destroy the temple or the priesthood, but only trying to give the Jewish people hope in these desperate times.

Inside the garden gates, Yahshua looked at the four men and said,

"I am going to wander the grounds and meditate. Please stay here and watch for me, for now I need to be alone."

"We will stand watch, Master." Judas answered.

He watched as Yahshua made his way down the path through the garden. Each of the men spread out their cloaks and sat on the ground to wait. Judas watched as each leaned against the walls of the gates and fell quickly asleep. Judas was fighting drowsiness himself and promised himself that he was only going to rest his eyes, but soon was sleeping also.

"So none of you could stay awake?" Yahshua's voice roused him from his sleep.

His eyes adjusting to the dark, he saw laughter around his Master's eyes and knew then he was not upset with his sleeping guard. As the others got to their feet, Judas heard a commotion from outside the gates. Turning toward the opening, he saw a regimen of Roman Guards advancing toward the gates.

"We must hide you, Master." he said to Yahshua taking him by the arms and trying to lead him away quickly.

"No, Judas, no. It is time to face this. I will not be a man who runs and cowers."

"But Master..." John's voice said in a hushed tone, "These are the Romans."

Peter drew his sword, "No Master, I will not let them take you."

"Put away your sword, Peter. It will do no good." Yahshua said quietly.

Judas watched as members of the guard approached Yahshua.

"We have an arrest warrant for you," the guard said, taking his arm. "You have been charged with crimes against Rome and crimes against Judea. Take him."

Several guardsmen surrounded Yahshua.

"You have the wrong man. The man you want is Barabbas." Judas yelled at the man who appeared to be in charge. "This man has done nothing."

"If he has done nothing, he has nothing to fear." the guard replied. "We have Barabbas in custody also. My orders are to take both to Pilot. Rome will judge these two men."

"I tell you..." Judas began.

"I tell you, if you do not wish to share his fate, leave now."

Yahshua looked at the four men, "Go now. Judas you know what you have to do. All of you go."

The guard began marching forward, surrounding Yahshua so there was no chance of escape.

The four men stood and watched the regimen leave, confusion on all of their faces. Peter turned.

"You did this. You gave Yahshua to the Romans. I saw you talking to Caiaphas. You told him he would be here, didn't you?"

Judas took a deep breath. How could he have

been so wrong about the high priest? He had indeed betrayed his master, but was not going to admit that to Peter.

"You know nothing." He spat into Peter's face. "What I know is that we must come up with some way to save Yahshua."

Judas stormed out the gates in the direction the Roman Guard had gone. As he got a hold of his own emotions, he realized that Yahshua had suspected this was going to happen. He recalled Yahshua's words when he had told him about the meeting with Caiaphas,

"If it is God's will I talk to this man, then so be it. If not, then God's will be done."

If only Yahshua had shared with him his suspicions, then Judas could have been better prepared and the arrest would have never happened. Now, he had no choice but to make his wrong decision right again.

Having been with his father to Pilot's palace many times, Judas knew that Pilot would do nothing before morning. Morning, Passover or not, Pilot would hear the case against both men and make his judgment. Judas knew he had to be there when he did, but to arrange the plan he had begun to formulate in his mind, he would have to make sure his father was not at the palace to save his own son from death.

* * *

Right now, he had to enlist help and tell the women all that had transpired. Judas headed back to the Inn. James and John would be there by now, and once he had talked to the women, he would convince them of what he needed them to do to save Yahshua from the pike pole of the Romans.

109

He found Miriam weeping uncontrollably upon entering the room.

"She's been like that since the others returned." Mary said. "What has happened?"

"They did not tell you?" he asked.

"They told us nothing."

"Yahshua has been arrested. Barabbas also. They will be taken before Pilot in the morning."

"What are we to do, Judas?" Miriam asked between sobs.

"I have a plan, but I will need much help to pull it off."

"I'll do whatever I have to in order to save my husband." Miriam said.

"I also." replied Mary.

"Here is what I wish from you. Rome has traditionally pardoned a criminal of the Jews choice on the Passover. There will be a large crowd outside the palace in the morning. Somehow, get the people to chant for the release of Barabbas."

"Barabbas? Why?" Miriam asked, "How will that save my husband?"

"Your husband will be released in the place of Barabbas. Pilot will believe that Yahshua is my brother."

"But why not just chant for the release of Yahshua?" Mary asked.

"Because Caiaphas is convinced that Yahshua is a threat. He will only seek to have him arrested once again, after Passover."

"You are sure you can do this? Pull off such a deceit with Pilot?" Miriam asked.

"The two are so much alike, Pilot will not be able to know the difference between them. I alone will be there to identify my brother."

"But what of our father? Surely he will hear of what has happened and will try and intervene for Barabbas."

"I, with the help of John and James, will make sure my father does not make it to the palace until all is said and done. We will save him Miriam. Now I must go, there is much work to be done before first light. Be at the palace at dawn, everything depends on you and the crowd."

"We will be there, Judas." Mary said.

Miriam nodded, "May the Goddess protect us all and may she give us all the strength needed to accomplish this task. We will be there before light, Judas, and do as you have asked."

Chapter Twenty

The night had passed swiftly since he had left the women with much left to do to set his plan into action. The hardest part of the plan had been to convince Peter to stay at the Inn and await word of Yahshua's fate, while getting James and John alone to let them know their part.

After leaving the Inn, he made his way back to his father's villa, waiting outside the garden gates for John and James to arrive. John arrived first.

"Peter is suspicious. I do not know if James got away without him following or not." John said, "But I know I was not followed."

"We'll give James a few more minutes and if he does not arrive, we'll do what needs to be accomplished alone." Judas replied.

James arrived breathlessly a few minutes later. "Peter thinks I've gone to relieve myself." he said with a slight chuckle.

"Are you sure he didn't follow you?" Judas asked.

"I'm sure. I went through the Roman marketplace. It was easy to get lost in the crowds there."

"You each know what we have to do?" Judas asked.

"You really think we must do this to save Yahshua?" John asked.

"I see no other way. I am sure my father has been notified that both Yahshua and Barabbas have been arrested. We must keep him away from the palace, or my plan will be meaningless."

"Let's get it done and over, then." James said.

The three men entered the villa garden. No lamps appeared to be burning from within the house. They entered and Judas led them down the hallways to his father's chambers.

As quietly as possible, Judas lifted the latch on the chamber door. Inside the room, he could make out his father's sleeping form in the bed. Silently, Judas crossed the room and placed his hand over the older man's mouth. James and John came up to either side of the bed. John produced rope from beneath his tunic and with the help of James, bound the man's arms behind his back. A scarf was produced and Judas used it as a gag.

"Father, we are taking you with us. We will not harm you. When I have secured Yahshua's freedom, you will be released." Judas' eyes were cold as he stared into his father's face, "If you try to escape and make any sound on the way out of this villa, I will kill you. Do you understand?"

Judas saw the fear in his father's eyes as he slowly nodded his head.

"You trained me well, father. It is too bad that you disowned me or my decisions may have been different."

James and John helped the older man from the bed and onto his feet. Judas stood behind his father and grabbed the rope binding his hands, twisting as he pushed him toward the door.

"Remember, Father, one hand holds your binds; the other holds a blade."

As silently as they had entered, the three men led their charge away from the villa and to a room Judas had secured close by. The darkness covered their path and they were seen by no one along the way.

Inside the room, the three men secured Joseph

to a heavy chair.

"James will keep you company, Father, until I or John return with news."

Judas turned to James, "As soon as I can, I will return. Until then, keep him bound and keep him gagged."

James nodded, "Save our Master. That is all that matters now."

Judas motioned to John, "Let's go, you know what you need do next."

The two men left and made their way separately toward Pilot's palace.

Judas arrived at the Roman palace before dawn, tired and weary. He waited until sunrise to knock on the palace doors.

"I was sent by my father, Joseph of Arimathea." He said to the servant who opened the door.

The servant nodded, "Pilot is expecting you, or rather, he was expecting your father."

"My father could not be here." Judas replied.

The servant led him to Pilot's Great Hall. The doors to the great balcony had not yet been opened. He was in time, he thought, saying a thank you prayer to God. Yet as he entered the room, he saw two bodies lying upon the floor, both badly beaten and bloody. His heart sank, *were they both dead?* he wondered as he walked toward them.

Moments later, Pilot entered the room and a servant opened the balcony doors.

"Where is your father?" Pilot demanded, "I sent for him."

"This morning, my father could not be found. But this note was left."

Judas handed him a note, in his father's hand, stating that he, Judas was to have the final word in this matter. Pilot had no way of knowing the note had been written years before in regards to a business matter his father had sent him to attend.

"So be it." Pilot said.

Outside, the voices of the people begin to ring into the large chamber.

In unison, the voices were crying. "Clemency, for Passover. Clemency, It's Passover."

"Get them to their feet," he said to the guards, "Bring them to the balcony. Tradition insists I must release one of them, let them choose which one. I wash my hands of this whole matter."

Pilot walked out onto the balcony facing the throng of people chanting below. He raised his arms and the people slowly silenced. The guards dragged the two broken men onto the balcony to either side of Pilot.

"Clemency, it's Passover." The voices began again.

"Choose," Pilot's voice boomed over the crowd, "Choose!"

At first, it appeared the voices were divided, half calling for the pardon of Yahshua the other half calling for the pardon of Barabbas. Within minutes, the voices became one, Barabbas was chosen by the people for the Passover pardon.

"Barabbas will go free; this one who thinks he is King of the Jews and the Son of God will die on the pole." Pilot made his pronouncement then turned and reentered the great hall.

"I cannot tell these two apart." Pilot said, "That is why I called for your father."

Inwardly, Judas relaxed, this was going better than he had hoped.

"Kiss your brother, Judas and he shall go free."

"Although they are badly beaten, I will know

him by his eyes," Judas responded, "My brother's eyes are blue."

"Open your eyes!" Pilot ordered the two beaten men.

Judas stood and watched as the guards pulled both men's heads back with their hair. In the eyes of Barabbas, he saw betrayal; in the eyes of Yahshua, he saw thankfulness. Judas walked to Yahshua and kissed him on the cheek.

"This is my brother." he said solemnly.

"Then take him and go." Pilot said.

The guard threw the broken body of Yahshua toward Judas. Judas caught him before he again hit the floor and wrapping his arm around him, began leading him away. Behind him, he could hear Pilot talking to his brother,

"So you wish to be a king? King of the Jews?" Pilot didn't wait for an answer, "So be it. Take him to Golgotha."

Judas turned to watch as the guards began dragging Barabbas toward him. His brother looked at him and smiled, "I will be the Messiah. Father should have chosen me for this, I have accomplished the task that he could not."

Judas could see the insanity in his brother's eyes.

"I am the Messiah." Barabbas began screams as they continued to drag him down the hallway.

So this was the plan his father had for Yahshua, the plan he was never totally privy to, Judas thought as he led Yahshua away from the palace. His father had planned all along to sacrifice Yahshua to fulfill the ancient prophecy of a messiah. Now he would lose his only son.

John was waiting at the appointed place with a

donkey and cart along with Miriam, her infant son and Mary. With their help, they laid Yahshua into the straw in the back and covered him with a soft linen sheet.

"Go now to Damascus. The rooms are already waiting. Stay there until the rest of us arrive."

"Judas, thank you." Miriam said, weeping.

"Go, I'll see you in a few days' time. There is much to do here yet."

John urged the cart forward and Judas watched them until they were out of sight before making his way back to the room where his father was being held.

Entering the room, he looked at his father with contempt.

"Your son is being crucified as we speak." He said, hatred dripping from his words.

"Yahshua is safe, as are his wife and son. Now you will have to live with what your quest for glory has befallen you."

Judas crossed the room and removed the gag from his father's mouth.

The older man licked his lips a few times before speaking, "You betrayed your own brother for Yahshua?" he asked.

"I did." Judas answered simply.

"You will be a wanted man. I shall tell Pilot of your deceit."

"It will do you no good, Father. I gave him enough proof that he will not believe that you did not send me to do the task of choosing which was Barabbas. Pilot will only believe that you are trying to deceive him now. Your fate is sealed, Father. Either you are with us or not."

"What proof is that?"

"That does not matter. Anything you can say to Pilot, I can counter. One word that he has killed the wrong man, and he will kill you. Pilot cannot allow for mistakes, it would undermine his power here. You know that as well as I."

Judas watched as Joseph slumped in his chair. He was broken now, Judas thought, he knows the truth of my words.

"At least, allow me to go to Pilot to claim the body. Yahshua was my nephew, he will not deny me that."

"I will allow that, Father, provided I come with you. One false word and I will kill you myself."

The older man only nodded as James undid the ropes binding him to the chair.

Judas looked at James, "You know where to meet. Go tell Peter all that has happened. Travel separately, so not to attract any attention. I will see you soon."

James nodded and left. Judas escorted his father to Pilot's palace for what he hoped would be his last time there. Inside, a note sent to Pilot asking for the body was granted and both men made their way to the Golgotha hill outside the city gates. They found Barabbas hanging between two other men. Over his head was a plaque inscribed simply, "King of the Jews".

Crucifixion was a slow death, but looking at Barabbas as he was being heckled by the Jewish mob, Judas didn't believe they would have long to wait. The two men stood to the side, as the crowd teased the man with barbs.

"If you are the son of God, get down."

"Why doesn't God save you?"

Another group stood on the other side of the mob, openly crying. These followers of Yahshua did not know their Master has escaped this fate. They

118

would never know the truth.

The Roman guards protecting the pike poles kept attempting to push the mob back. After thirty minutes of pushing, one soldier took his sword and ran it threw the side of Barabbas.

"It is accomplished." the guard said in a loud voice. "There is nothing more for you here today. Go home."

The crowd on the side of the hill mumbled for a few minutes longer, then slowly began to disperse. When none of the angry crowd remained, Joseph handed the order to the guard from Pilot allowing him to remove the body.

With Barabbas' body between them and the Yahshua's faithful followers behind them, Judas and his father carried the dead man to Joseph's private tomb and laid the body on an empty slab. The women immediately entered the tomb and began cleaning the body, finally wrapping it in a linen shroud.

Judas waited until the women had completed their work. When the last had left the tomb, he and his father rolled the tombstone back into place over the opening. Judas saw tears in his father's eyes and his heart began to soften.

"I am sorry it came to this, Father." he said as they walked away from the tomb and the mourners surrounding it.

"What is done, is done." Joseph said. "Where do you go from here?"

"I cannot tell you that, Father. Surely you understand why."

"I do. None of us is safe now. If Pilot ever learns of your duplicity, he will kill us all. It is best we all get away from Jerusalem at the moment."

"Where will you go?" Judas asked.

"I will finish what business I need to here and then your mother and I will go to Alexandria, to my house there."

"Alexandria is still under the control of Rome, do you think it will be safe?"

"Safe enough, I believe." Joseph nodded, "If not, I'll return to Britain."

Judas realized at that moment what the cost had been to his father. He had lost everything now, his son, his nephew and his standing in the community here.

"Father, I am sorry."

"As I said, what is done is done. If you, or my nephew, need safe passage away, meet me in Alexandria. I'll have a ship at the ready for you."

"Thank you, Father. Let us hope none of us needs it."

Chapter Twenty One

Miriam cried as she cleaned Yahshua's wounds. The cat o'nine tails had laid open deep crevices upon his back and from the bruising on his body, it was obvious he had been beaten by more than one man. As John drove the cart slowly toward Damascus, Miriam was thankful he appeared to go out of his way to keep the drive smooth and avoid the potholes in the weatherworn roadway.

Yahshua had opened his eyes several times during the trip, giving Miriam weak smiles before drifting back into unconsciousness. Miriam listened carefully to his breathing and they drove for miles before she was assured that he would live. It would take months for him to fully recover, but after checking his body as best as her limited healing techniques allowed, she felt confident that he had escaped death. This time at least.

Darkness approached when they finally arrived at the Inn at Damascus. John went inside to search for Nathanael to help carry Yahshua's body to the rooms, while the women covered his body with a new clean linen cloth. Miriam had to smile when Mary reminded her what type of picture it would present to carry him into the inn in a bloody sheet. Within moments, John and Nathaniel returned and carried the unconscious man into a well-furnished room in the inn.

As Miriam tended her husband, she listened to the conversation between the two men. Nathaniel was full of questions, wanting to know what had happened in Jerusalem. As John filled in the details that he knew, Miriam realized how close they had come to losing Yahshua to the pole.

"But why the deception?" Nathaniel asked, "I'm sure Pilot would have freed either. Why not have the crowd plead for Yahshua's life?"

"Judas believes that the Jews would still want him dead. Barabbas was no threat to the priesthood, in fact, in many ways contributed to the priest's plans." John replied.

"So what's next?" Nathaniel asked.

"We wait here for the others. We wait for Judas; he'll know what to do next. However, I can guess, we'll have to leave Judea. I don't think it's safe here for any of us now."

"Will they be here soon?"

"In the next day or two, I'm sure. I know Judas had to bury his brother and I'm sure he will try to make amends with his father."

"What does my father have to do with this?" Miriam asked.

"To make his plan work, Judas held his father hostage, while he went to the palace. Had your father went to Pilot, the chances are very good Yahshua would be dead now. Joseph of Arimathea would have indeed saved his own son first."

"But he loved Yahshua." Miriam protested.

"He loved his son more. He was only using Yahshua to accomplish his own goals. He wasn't going to risk his own son."

"His own goals? What...?" Miriam's voice trailed off. She looked over at Mary whose eyes showed the betrayal that she also felt.

"He planned for Yahshua to be the next Messiah of the people. To fulfill the Psalms, he knew Yahshua had to die."

Miriam looked down at her sleeping husband, brushing a stray hair from his face. She had known her father was cold and callous, but had no idea he could be this calculating. She wondered what he had hoped to gain. Was it more power and wealth? It seemed he already had more than enough to satisfy any man.

Her thoughts were interrupted by James entering the room.

"Well?" John asked.

"Barabbas is dead. Pilot waited little time hanging him from the pole."

"And Judas?" Nathaniel asked.

"He will be along as soon as he ties up loose ends."

"Peter?"

"I'm sure he'll be along soon. I stopped by the old rooms and told him to meet us here. I would have preferred to leave him behind."

"I too," John and Nathaniel said in unison.

"I'll go see and if I can round up some food." John said. He returned a few minutes later carrying a tray laden with a tureen of thick soup and bowls along with several loaves of heavy bread.

The innkeeper brought up several pitchers of wine along with cups to drink with. "Can I be of any further service?" he inquired.

"It is enough for now." John said, dismissing the small man.

When they were all alone in the room again, Nathaniel asked,

"That kind of service must have cost a small fortune."

"Judas gave me plenty of coins. Just for this type of thing. We have the entire Inn to ourselves now. Might I suggest now that we have eaten, we retire to separate rooms? I'm sure the women would like to get some much needed rest."

The men stood. "I'll stay in the tavern near the entry, in case the others show up. That way you won't be disturbed tonight."

"Thank you John. Thank you for everything."

"What I did, I did for my Master." John said before he went out the door, closing it behind him.

Miriam went back to her husband's side, wondering what part John had played in Judas' plot to save Yahshua. Was he now a wanted man also?

Chapter Twenty Two

After his brother was in the tomb, Judas turned his attention back to his father. Although the older man now seemed broken, having lost both Barabbas and Yahshua, Judas did not trust him to let the matter lie. From a distance, he followed his father back to the villa with the intention of watching his actions for at least several days or until he was sure Joseph would not go to Pilot with the truth of the deception.

His mind changed as he watched from the shadows of the villa gardens a lone man creep from behind the villa and make his escape into the streets of the city. Judas rushed into the house to find his father hovered over his mother's bloody body. A single knife wound in her chest. Around the room, several servants lay on the floor also, blood pooling around their bodies.

"We can do no good for her here, father." Judas said, his voice uneven.

"Why?" Joseph looked up at his son, his dead wife cradled in his lap.

"I don't know why." Judas answered as honestly as he could, "maybe a few of Barabbas' followers recognized him today. But it is not safe for you here any longer, the assassin will return."

"So where do I go? I'm not prepared for a journey to Alexandria now."

"Come with me, Father. We will go to Yahshua."

Judas reached down and took his father by the shoulders.

"Come, let us collect what is needed and leave this place."

If Judas had any doubts about his father being a

broken man, they dissipated as he led the man toward his chambers and helped him pack a travel satchel.

"Your money, Father, where do you keep it?"

At first, Joseph seemed not to understand the question, then finally answered,

"If you tip the bedstead over, you will find the posts hollow. There is money in each hollow post."

Judas threw the down mattress to the floor and laid the bedstead over on its side. Each of the four main posts were stuffed with small leather pouches of both Jewish and Roman coin. Each pouch was attached to the next one within the pole. Knowing that he would not be able to hide the pouches on his person, Judas reached for a second traveling bag lying empty where the bed had stood.

"Is there more in the house?" he asked, looking again at his father.

Joseph nodded, "The legs of my writing table in the salon are the same."

"Finish packing," Judas said. He took the satchel and with a knife drawn, made his way slowly toward the salon. The contents from the writing desk filled the satchel and with effort, Judas tied the bag closed and went back for his father.

"Are you ready, Father?"

"I have no choice." Joseph replied.

"Then let us leave now, before it becomes too late."

Joseph nodded and began following Judas to the door. They made their way through the villa without being seen and Judas suspected the rest of the servants had either run off or were dead also.

Leaving the gardens, Judas watched as his father turned and looked for the last time at the villa he had built. Pity sprang in his heart for the old man as he saw a single tear stream down his cheek. Judas didn't know whether the tear was for his dead wife or the life he was leaving behind.

Judas joined the group three days later bringing with him his father, Joseph of Arimathea. Jerusalem was no longer safe for any of them, as zealots had stolen the body of Barabbas from the tomb and were indeed proclaiming a risen Christ.

Yahshua was now awake and healing from his wounds. While he still could not walk without help, he was able to sit up and talk to his followers. Miriam tried not to hover over him as he healed and Mary busied herself with the day-to-day tasks at hand of caring for such a large group of men.

Peter had arrived shortly after Judas. He made his dissatisfaction of being left out of all that had happened in Jerusalem known.

"You don't trust me." he said flatly to Judas over dinner.

"You are right, I don't." Judas had answered just as flat.

"I should have been included." Peter replied.

Judas stood and stared at Peter. "I, alone, with my Master, make the decisions of protecting this group. I will answer to no one except Yahshua. Are we clear on this, Peter?"

"Who put you in charge?" Peter asked defiantly.

"I did." Yahshua said from the opposite end of the table. "If it were not for the tactics of Judas, I would be a dead man now. Judas is in charge, now and for as long as we are together. If anyone has a problem with that, they are free to leave now."

Miriam watched as Peter stared first at Yahshua and then at Judas before sitting back down at the table.

Her instincts told her that it was only a matter of time before Peter betrayed them all.

"As soon as you are well enough, we must leave here, Master." Judas said.

A chorus from the others, "Where do we go?" met his statement.

"I have a house in Alexandria." Joseph said, "It is large enough for all of us and far away enough from the happenings in Judea to be safe, I think."

"Again, we cannot travel together." Judas said, "We must break into small groups, no more than two men and their families."

"I will leave tomorrow to make the house ready," Joseph said, "Allow me two weeks and I will have all secured."

"Then it is decided." Judas said, "We will begin dispersing before the end of the week and meet back in Alexandria."

"It is decided." Yahshua affirmed, looking straight at Peter. Miriam thought his look was almost a dare to defy him.

The meal ended and the men went to the other rooms. Only Judas remained with the women with Yahshua.

"Can we trust our father?" She asked Judas when they were alone.

"Our father has a large fortune to lose if he doesn't disappear for a while, Miriam. His plans of glory may be gone, but he is not fool enough to lose everything."

"Is Alexandria truly far enough?" Miriam asked.

"I don't know." Judas responded and Miriam could hear the honesty in his voice. "We will decide what next we must do after we arrive. We may have to flee from there also. It all depends on Rome, now."

Over the next few days, Judas sent out the disciples and their families in small parties to make the trip overland to Alexandria. Yahshua continued to recover and was soon well enough to travel himself. When the last of the group had been gone three days, Judas decided it was time for them to make the journey. They left at dark, hoping to be far from Jerusalem by morning.

Chapter Twenty Three

Miriam had difficulties being in her father's house in Alexandria. No longer banished to the kitchens, she enjoyed free reign over her comings and goings, as well as the servants. Remembering how she had been treated, she rarely asked any of them to provide for her what she could provide for herself.

When first arriving in the city, the entire group had stayed within the walls of Joseph's home and gardens. As the days passed, many found work and other lodgings, so now all that remained besides herself and family, were John and Peter. John helped Joseph and Judas on the docks when ships would come, while Peter did little but listen to local gossip concerning the events in Jerusalem.

Each evening during the communal meal, Peter made a point to let the others know exactly what was happening back home.

"I've heard a new zealot by the name of Saul has been preaching of a risen Christ." Peter said one evening while taking a sip of wine. "Says he's had a conversion and is no longer trying to kill Christ's followers. Going by the new name of Paul."

"I've heard of him." Yahshua said, "He's a fool."

"Fool or not, he is gaining followers." Peter replied, "Mostly those we left behind."

"If they cannot discern between truth and lies," Judas began, "it is best they were left behind."

"But this Paul is distorting the truth. We know Yahshua didn't die. He needs to stop spreading lies."

"Oh and do you plan on setting him straight,

Peter?" Judas asked, "Only because the Romans believe Yahshua to be dead is he safe."

"What care we what lies are told?" Yahshua asked.

Peter looked at the two men, "They are using your name. Saying you are the new Messiah of the Jewish race. Doesn't that bother you?"

"They are also saying I was born of a virgin." Yahshua said laughing, "We both know that is not true."

Mary, who rarely said anything when the others were present, laughed, "I think I can confirm that."

Everyone around the table laughed except for Peter. Miriam watched as he sat back, a frown upon his face as he peered into his wine cup. The talk moved to other things and Miriam busied herself with cleaning the face and hands of her young son before setting him from her lap onto the floor to play.

Soon she would have to tell Yahshua she was again with child. As she had been unable to find the herbs she needed in this environment to prevent conception, she hoped that he would indeed be happy to be a father once more. Yet she wasn't sure. Even though life had settled into a routine here, Yahshua had seemed hardened, more withdrawn since the events in Jerusalem.

Miriam couldn't blame him. He had been betrayed and beaten to near death and only by the sacrificing of his cousin had he been allowed to live. She knew that he felt betrayed also by Joseph, a man he had looked to almost as a father. Yahshua, as well as herself, knew the fate that had fallen Barabbas was the fate intended by Joseph for him. Had it not been for Judas' intervention, Yahshua would have been the subject of all of Peter's gossip.

The meal completed, Miriam rose to help Mary gather the dishes. Mary, like herself, attempted to save the servants extra work, much to Joseph's chagrin. Yet because of the women's willingness to help out, the staff could be kept to a bare minimum. Judas felt this was for the best as the less people around, the less chance of the truth being revealed would be.

For now, Miriam would have to accept what Judas said. Even above her father, Judas' word was now considered law among the followers.

Chapter Twenty Four

Judas walked into the small shed Yahshua had claimed after they had arrived in Alexandria. Woodworking tools were scattered everywhere, on benches, the floor and on partially finished pieces.

In the center of the shed, Yahshua was bent over a large circular tabletop carefully chiseling away small sections of the sanded boards. Judas found an empty section of dirt floor and lowered his body into a sitting position.

"Peter grows restless, Master." he said.

"I fear Peter will always be restless." Yahshua replied, "He misses his home, he misses those things that he thought he would accomplish with me."

"Can we still trust him, Yahshua? I cannot help but wonder."

"Peter wants only to be where the action is. I fear we have become too staid, too normal, for his liking. He hears of the happenings in Judea and longs to be a part of them."

"Are you suggesting sending him back there?" Judas asked, afraid to hear the answer.

"He would make a good spy." Yahshua said with a laugh. "Through him, we could discover the truth and not have to listen to idle gossip."

Judas sat back against the wall, thinking as he watched Yahshua take a light colored piece of wood and fit it into the slot he had chiseled out on the tabletop.

"I don't know about you, Judas, but I am indeed curious to know what happened to Barabbas' body. Was he stolen by my followers or by his fellow zealots?

I would like to know who, if anyone, knows the truth in Jerusalem."

"You speak wisely, Master." Judas said after long thought. "Peter could possibly find this out. But do you not think one of the other's would be better suited to the task?"

"I know you don't trust him, Judas. I know also that Miriam does not either. I'm not even sure I do, but this would be a test. And I do not propose to send him alone; I plan to send Matthew back as well. Not together, but with one watching the other."

"Master, your mind is more devious than mine." Judas said with a laugh. "Do you think Matthew will be willing?"

"Matthew will do anything I ask. His family still lives outside the city, he will be glad to see them. Once we discover the truth, he can rejoin us then."

"When do you mean for this to happen?" Judas asked.

"Soon. I will talk to Peter in a day or so. First, we will talk to Matthew. Make sure he understands the trust and duties we are placing upon him."

"How do you plan to get Matthew away from the others, especially Peter?"

"Leave that to me. I will contrive some reason to have Matthew stay behind after supper or will instigate an argument so Peter will storm out. We both know, either you or Miriam can regularly cause him to do that."

"It is unfortunate, but ultimately true, Master. I fear there is no love lost between either of us and Peter."

"As it should be, Judas, as it should be."

Judas rose to leave as Yahshua continued with his work. Judas could now begin to see the star pattern

134

forming in the tabletop. When Yahshua had this completed, the table would be beautiful beyond words. So far, there had been no mention of selling his work, and Judas wondered what plans Yahshua had for the table. For now, he would save that question for later.

Chapter Twenty Five

For the Sabbath, the group met together at
Joseph's home. Gathered around a large table in the
dining hall, they talked among themselves about the
day-to-day things that had occurred during the past
week. Rumors were coming faster now about the
unrest in Jerusalem, where the followers of the new
Christ were being persecuted by both the Romans and
the Jewish priests.

"I hope your friend at the Temple will not suffer
because of this?" Yahshua said to Miriam.

"I do fear for her, not only because of the unrest,
but also her role when we rescued you." Miriam
answered.

Suddenly, Peter's voice boomed across the
room,

"Do you really need to discuss the heathens at
the Sabbath dinner? With her?"

"Miriam is my wife and my most beloved
disciple, Peter. What is the problem?"

"Only you allow children and women to eat
with the men, only you divulge confidences to the
womenfolk."

"That is the way it is, Peter. It is how I do
things. Have you never listened to my words, Peter? I
practice only what I teach. All are equal before God."

Miriam could see the anger rise in Peter's face.
With what appeared to be deliberate action, he laid the
knife in his hand on the table. His lips moved, as if to
say something further, then instead he turned and left
the room.

Yahshua nodded to Judas, then said to Miriam,

"I had best go smooth his ruffled feathers."

Her dislike of Peter was so intense, Miriam smiled, as she couldn't help but feel some satisfaction in his public rebuke.

Yahshua left the table to follow Peter, Miriam knew it was all part of a plan that would leave Judas able to talk to Matthew alone about returning to Jerusalem. Yahshua had promised her that Matthew would check after Mircalla also when he returned to the city and if she was in need to send her here.

Miriam wasn't as convinced as Yahshua and Judas that Peter would return from Jerusalem. He obsessed over his interest of this Paul and the so-called risen Christ. If he failed to return, she felt the entire group would be better served. Miriam put the thoughts out of her mind and returned to eating her meal and talking with the others. Time alone would tell soon enough, if Peter would go and if he would complete the task his master was giving him now.

Chapter Twenty Six

Judas and Yahshua had locked themselves behind closed doors with Joseph and Matthew. Matthew had returned earlier in the day from Jerusalem saying that Peter would soon follow, but he had felt it unsafe to remain there any longer. After a short nap and a meal, the men had sequestered themselves here to learn of the happenings in Judea.

"Paul is stirring up the masses. He is indeed saying that you are the risen Christ, the new Messiah of Israel."

"How many followers does he have?" Judas asked.

"In Jerusalem alone, several thousand," Matthew answered, "in the whole of Judea, ten times that."

"I don't imagine Caiaphas is happy about that?" Yahshua said.

"Caiaphas is intensely angry, the Zealots have sworn that they will kill anyone who follows Paul and Caiaphas has sanctioned the Zealots."

"And Rome?" Yahshua asked.

"Rome is crucifying Christians daily. Some days as many as a dozen."

"Did you hear any mention of us?" Judas asked.

"Constantly, everywhere I went, I was questioned about you, Judas and your father. Pilot is searching for both of you. I told the guard I had last seen you when Yahshua was crucified."

"You did well." Judas said, "Obviously they believed you or you would not have been allowed free. You were not followed back here?"

"No, I don't think so. I saw few people on the road, so I believe I traveled alone."

"Tell us of Peter." Yahshua said.

"Peter immediately joined Paul's followers on arriving in Jerusalem. Anytime you saw Paul, Peter was at his side."

"So Paul trusts him?" Judas asked.

"It would appear so. I think Peter is enamored with the thought of the risen Christ. He, too, was preaching wherever he could find an audience."

Judas watched as Yahshua's brow furrowed, and asked Matthew,

"Surely he doesn't believe that? I mean, after all, he knows the truth."

"It sounded like he believed; he was preaching that Yahshua had said that 'he' would be the rock his church was founded on. But it may be, he just wanted the power, the glory and the homage the masses were giving him."

"So why is he returning here? Surely he is receiving what he wants in Jerusalem."

Judas could hear the anger in Yahshua's voice.

"According to the people I talked to, Peter and Paul had a huge argument. Almost coming to blows. Paul said there could not be two leaders of the New Christians and that Peter needed to step back as he, Paul, had begun this. Peter refused, saying that he had been closer to you in life, therefore he deserved to lead the people."

Judas rose from his chair and began pacing the room, as Matthew continued,

"Paul told Peter to leave Jerusalem, to leave Judea, that he could not be responsible for his safety. It was little more than a veiled threat. That was when Peter acquiesced and said he would take his ministry to

Egypt and the nations west of Judea. After more arguing, Paul agreed, telling Peter that Judea and all lands east belong to him."

"So will Paul hold to his bargain?" Yahshua asked.

"No." Came the simple answer from Joseph, who until now had been quiet. "Saul of Tarsus is much like me; he will not simply give over power without a fight. Name change or not, he is still a Zealot and a skilled assassin."

"Then you think he will follow Peter?" Yahshua asked.

"Either he, or some Zealot mercenary." Joseph said.

"Paul knows that you are alive, also, Master." Matthew said, "I do not know how he knows, but he does. And he knows about Miriam and the children."

"Did Peter betray us to him?" Yahshua asked, the anger in his voice seething just under the surface.

"I do not know, Master. I only heard mention of them from one of Paul's followers."

"We are no longer safe here." Judas said. "We must begin making plans to disperse once again."

"At least we have a little time." Yahshua said.

"We'll go to Gaul," Joseph said, "I have a small house there also."

Judas looked at Yahshua who appeared lost in thought, "I think we need to split up for a short while, some of us going one way, the rest another."

"And Peter, what do we do with him if he returns?" Joseph asked.

"He will go to Gaul with you." Judas answered, "I trust you to keep an eye on him, Father."

"Where will you go?" Joseph asked.

"Those of us who are single, along with

Yahshua, will go to India. We will be safe there. Those who have families will go with you."

"Miriam isn't going to like this plan." Yahshua said with a small laugh, "especially since it is close to time for her delivery."

"You'll have to make her understand, cousin." Judas said softly, "For the safety of both you and her children, it is best to split up. I will send John with them to be their personal protector."

"Make it so," Yahshua said to the men around the table. "How soon can you have a ship ready to sail, Uncle?"

"In less than a weeks' time." Joseph replied.

"Then we will be ready then, also. And if Peter has not returned, you will sail without him, do not wait."

"I'd just as soon leave him behind." Joseph said.

"I know, Uncle. But I may have need of him in the future."

"There is much to be done," Judas interrupted, "It is best, Master that you be gone before Peter returns."

"I agree, Judas. I'll go break the news to Miriam and my mother. You can fill the others in as needed."

Chapter Twenty Seven

The early morning sun blazed radiant heat down on the already scorching sands of the Egyptian desert. Two figures stood alone, inches apart, and seemed in the light to be only glimmers in the shadows of the dunes.

"I want to go with you." The woman said with a plaintive look on her face.

"Where I go, you cannot follow, Miriam. It is not safe." The man answered, attempting to be gentle and reassuring.

"Father insists we go to Gaul. I do not understand why we cannot return to Avalon."

"Because they will look there for you first."

"Is he really such a threat?" she asked.

"Paul is a fanatic. He will do all in his power to destroy you, me, the children. Now he has many of the Zealots on his side. At least in that, both agree they want us dead. None of us is safe."

"Where will you go? Am I permitted to at least know where my husband is?"

"Timothy, Judas and I go to India. There we will stay until I feel it is safe. Then I will join you." He said, taking her into his arms for one last embrace.

The tears were flowing from her eyes as she responded, "I hope that it is soon, Yahshua. I hope it is soon."

"I have to go." He said, as he pulled away. "I love you." Then he left, disappearing rapidly over the sand.

Mary watched until the figure became a small speck, then with heavy heart, turned and walked back to the city. The trip was slow, because of not only the heat but also her size, and it was almost dusk when she entered the city gates. Tired and not paying attention, she ran into the woman hurrying from an alleyway.

Startled, she mumbled an apology. The woman turned.

"It is no problem." Recognition spread over both of their faces.

"Mircalla, you are here!"

"Miriam, it is good to see you."

"How is it you are not in Jerusalem?" Mary asked.

"After it was discovered I lied about the child, it was no longer safe for me. I came here rather than face the vengeance of Rome. But you, why are you here?"

"Like you, we are running. Have you not heard what happened? "

"I have heard much. About how your husband is the risen Christ. How he is this new god."

"He cannot be the risen Christ. How could that be so as he is not dead?

"I only know the tales that are being told."

"Mircalla, can we sit?" The younger woman said pointing toward a bench, "I will tell you the truth of it."

Full darkness had taken over by the time the story had been told. Mary knew the others would be worried, yet didn't care. There was a question burning in her mind now.

"Mircalla, have I been unfaithful to the goddess? Have I betrayed her because of what I am a part of now?"

"No child, no. The old ways are dying for us here. I see this new religion building around your husband and it will be the death of us. But the story of his virgin birth is as old as time."

"How does that make a difference, Mircalla? I don't understand."

"The Jewish God is a weak god. That is why they took our legends, our myths, and our truths. The Son of this God still comes from the mother. That is your destiny. To keep the mother alive through the son. Do you understand?"

"I think so. But will it be the same?"

"All gods are one, Miriam. This is just another face for the goddess. Think on that, Miriam and know that you can shape the future. Just as your husband has."

"I hope you are right, Mircalla."

"I know I am, child. Now go, there must be someone who will be worried after all this time."

"There are more that wish me dead."

"They fear you and your strength. Do not worry about them; just do as you know you must. The goddess will guide and protect you."

With that, Mircalla kissed the young woman on the cheek and turned to leave. "Just remember, Miriam, she is always with you."

Miriam smiled her heart lighter and then began the short trek back to her father's house where everything was being transferred to the boat her father had provided for their journey.

Miriam entered the house only to find everything in disarray. Several of those left behind by Judas and Yahshua's leaving were indeed concerned about her absence. John had sent men into the streets of Alexandria to search for her.

"I am sorry, John, I did not mean to cause such worry." she said, humbly.

"You are safe, all is well." John said, "We were only concerned for your safety."

"I know. I promise, I will not allow it to happen again." she smiled knowing that after today, she would have no one except this little group to talk to anyway. She left John in search of Mary to see what was left to be done to ready themselves and her son for the journey to Gaul. Instead, she found her father, as usual barking orders to a group of men who were moving the needed provisions to the boat. He turned and looked at her as she entered the room.

"Before we leave, Miriam, I need to talk to you." he said.

Very few words had been exchanged between the two of them since arriving in Alexandria and Miriam couldn't fathom what he had to say to her now.

"I need to ask your forgiveness." Joseph said simply.

Miriam looked at her father, after all he had put her through, after all he had put Yahshua through, now he wanted forgiveness?

Joseph took her by the arm, leading her to a small antechamber.

"Please, hear me out, daughter." he pleaded.

"I am listening, Father." she replied.

"In my quest for glory, I was misguided." He began, "I did believe that Yahshua could be the next Messiah of Israel, if he would follow my lead. I did not believe it could turn out this way. I had no intention of him, or anyone else, ending up on the end of a Roman pike pole. Only your brother could see what I could not."

"My brother? Who is my brother?" Miriam asked, not believing that it was possible that she had real family here.

"Judas is your brother. Born of your mother also."

Joseph continued to talk, but Miriam was no longer listening. It explained so much, why Judas had been so protective of her and the children, why she had been allowed to be included in the plans that had been made, both here and in Jerusalem.

"So my daughter, will you forgive a stupid old man?" Joseph asked, putting his hand on her shoulder.

Miriam looked at her father and saw tears streaming down his cheeks. Her heart softened,

"If my brother and my husband can forgive you Father, then I can also."

"Thank you, daughter. You have released a burden from my heart and from my mind." he said softly.

"Now, we must get back to the work at hand." Miriam said, "There is much left to do if we set sail tomorrow."

"There is indeed, daughter."

Miriam left the antechamber, again in search of her mother in law. She found her in the children's quarters attempting to put her now three-year-old son to bed. Young Joshua was giving Mary fits in his attempts to skip the bedtime ritual.

"Get in the bed child, now." Miriam said sternly.

The young boy looked at his mother and immediately climbed onto his small pallet and closed his eyes. The two women stood at the door for a few moments to make sure that he was indeed going to stay in bed. When Miriam saw his small chest rising and falling in sleep, she took Mary's arm and together the two women walked down the hallway.

"Did you know Judas was my brother?" Miriam asked.

"I suspected as much," Mary answered, "there is

much resemblance between the two of you. Did you never wonder?"

"No, not once. I knew he had Kelt blood, but never imagined that my mother had a son from Joseph also. My mother becomes more and more a mystery to me. I had thought I was only the result of a one-time occurrence."

"I remember when Joseph brought Judas here. He was a tiny thing, barely able to walk. Martha had tried for several years after the birth of Barabbas to have another child, but it wasn't to be. She claimed Judas as her own and most accepted that as Jewish women are very private about their maternity."

"You mean they hide it?"

"Yes, often. It is a source of embarrassment for many. It only becomes pride after the sons are born. I do believe had Joseph bought you here as a small child, she would have done the same with you. After a woman has produced sons, it is then acceptable to have a daughter."

"I am glad he didn't. I don't think I would have ever become a good Jewish woman, no matter who raised me." Miriam said with a laugh.

Miriam, you already are." Mary said laughing along with her daughter in law.

"Perish the thought," was the sentiment that ran through her mind, but she decided not to say the words aloud, not wanting to offend Mary.

"How much is left to do?" She said instead, changing the subject.

"Nothing more than collecting together our personal belongings. The things we want with us on the ship."

"I cannot imagine needing much." Miriam said, remembering her voyage from Avalon.

The two women parted at the doorways of their adjoining chambers.

"Father says he will awaken us early, I will be glad when this journey is done." Miriam said, her hand protectively on her large belly.

"I just hope he can wait until we arrive." Mary said.

"I do also." Miriam said.

She kissed her mother in law on the cheek and said, "I am so glad to have you with me, you have truly become my mother."

Mary hugged her in return, "And you, truly a daughter. Now go, sleep. I feel this will be our last good night of sleep for many days."

Miriam nodded and entered her chambers. They seemed empty without the presence of Yahshua. She sighed as she began gathering the last of her possessions and began putting them into the same traveling bag she had carried for her journey to Jerusalem so many years ago.

Chapter Twenty Eight

The boat to Gaul set sail from Alexandria at first light. Huddled in the cargo bay were forty people, including a very pregnant Miriam and her small son. With them were all their worldly belongings, including the large inlaid table that Yahshua had built while in Alexandria.

"Are you all right, Miriam?" Asked her father, "I am sorry the ship couldn't have been one of my larger ones, but it appears that Rome has seized them."

"I'm fine father. It is all right. Save your worry for the others, I think they will need it more." She responded.

As if on cue, a voice rang out, "Joseph, I'm going to be sick."

Taking his leave of her, Joseph went to the man who had called.

"No, Philip. You are not going to be sick. You have withstood much worse than this."

"It's just this rocking feeling, Joseph. And there is no air. No light. I feel as if I am going to suffocate."

"Just remember your option, Philip. Is this not better than assassination or crucifixion?"

"Yes, Joseph" the young man responded. "Anything is better than that."

Joseph turned and looked at the ragtag group in the cargo hold. He had paid more than two years earnings in the tin mines to finance this venture. Three weeks in this lightless cavern. Three weeks with barely enough room to move. Three weeks with very little food or fresh water. He thought about his daughter, Miriam. She would be delivered of her child in this stinking hellhole. "Father in heaven, let it be a son."

Joseph prayed silently to himself. Not only would another son be a source of pride for him, but the raising of the child, would allow Miriam a second boy child to dwell upon. Although he kept his fears to himself, Joseph felt she would never see her husband again.

Joseph knew Miriam had indeed forgiven him for the wrongs he had committed against her, yet he still felt that he owed her the best life he could give her from this point forward. He wished he could return her to the Isle, but Judas felt that would unsafe. He hoped that one day in the future, he would be able to make it right and return her back to the home she had loved.

Chapter Twenty Nine

The trip to Gaul had been difficult for everyone on board the small boat. Many of the small band had been stricken with dysentery and several of the children had died. Miriam had given birth to her son as the boat had rocked across high waves caused by a severe storm at sea a week before landing on the northern coast of Gaul.

The journey had been made worse by Peter's constant whining. Proselyting the new truth that Paul had shown him irritated the others. Miriam was too weary from seasickness, the pregnancy and the birth to argue with him, but had promised that once they were ashore she would find a way to reason with him and show him that what he was attempting to do was nothing less than betrayal to Yahshua.

For the time on the boat though, she relied on John to keep Peter as quiet as possible. When the first mate had shouted that land could be seen, everyone who was well enough made his or her way up from the cargo hold to the bow of the ship to watch the boat pull into the landing. Miriam smiled as she heard the loud cheers as the boat came to a slow stop.

Once docked, both John and her father came to her side.

"The others are making their way to land." her father said. "Here, lean on me, I'll help steady your steps."

Mary took the infant in her arms, while holding the hand of Joshua. Miriam allowed both Joseph and John to take her arms, drawing her to her feet. Faintness came over her as she became erect and she was glad of the support they gave on either side of her.

"I sent Phillip to procure a cart in the village." Joseph said, "It may not be the most comfortable, but it will get you to the house without walking."

Far better than the last cart I rode in with you, Miriam thought as the two men helped her in the small dingy that would take them to shore. Yet she bit her tongue as her father had been consolatory and even kind to her on this journey.

Once ashore, Phillip was waiting with a small donkey pulled cart filled with soft hay. The men helped Miriam into the back and joined Phillip on the small driver's seat. Mary and the two children joined Miriam in the back of the cart.

"It's only a short way from here." Joseph said, "We should have you in a proper bed soon."

Miriam smiled weakly at her father. "I am fine, Joseph. The others, will they follow us there?"

"Only for tonight. I'll arrange other lodgings for them tomorrow."

The cart made its way through the narrow streets of the village with Phillip following Joseph's directions. Miriam dozed, only to come awake as the cart stopped. Opening her eyes, she was surprised to see that her father's small house was more of a small castle, a fortress really with high walls and iron gates.

As the men helped her from the cart, she said with a weak laugh, "Not what I would call a small house, Father."

"I have only seen the place once," he replied, "I acquired it from a man who could not pay me what he owed. I had forgotten exactly what it looked like. It should serve us well until Yahshua and the others return."

"It should indeed." John said as they helped

Miriam inside and Phillip carried both her bag and Mary's into the castle.

"There's a salon to our right." Joseph said to John, "She can rest there until a room can be prepared for her and Mary."

John nodded. Once seated on a long upholstered settee, Joseph said, "I'll go see if I can find some fresh food for you and the child."

After he left the room, Miriam said, "My father has changed much."

"He is not the man I remember," Mary said, "But he has lost much, maybe now he understands the importance of family."

Within minutes, a servant entered the room carrying a tray laden with cheeses, meats and fruits. A second servant followed carrying large pitchers of wine and goblets. A smaller pitcher held fresh milk and a small cup for Joshua.

The days turned into weeks and as they settled into a routine, Miriam gained her strength back quickly. The new boy child, which Miriam named Abram as Yahshua had requested, was strong and grew quickly. Joshua was devoted to the infant and stayed close as possible to his new younger brother.

Joseph stayed true to his word and found lodging in the village for most of the followers who had joined them on the ship. Peter had been the hardest to get rid of, since he refused to understand why John was allowed to stay at the fortress and yet he was not. In the end, Joseph had had Peter's things packed up and two of the new bodyguards he had hired escorted the man to the rooms Joseph had acquired for Peter in the village.

Yet almost daily, Peter returned to ask if they had heard word from Yahshua. When he was not at the chateau, Phillip was charged with watching him and reporting back to either John or Joseph of his comings and goings. For Phillip it was an easy job as Peter loved to talk to anyone who would listen and was more than glad of his company. Thinking they were best friends, it was easy for Phillip to accompany Peter to the taverns were Peter constantly told the story of the newly risen Christ.

Over supper, several months after they had arrived in Gaul, Phillip asked the question that had been on everyone's mind.

"Do you think that Peter's mouth will bring the danger here?"

"I do wish I could find a way to shut him up." John said.

"This is what I was afraid of," Miriam added, "if anyone actually believes what he is saying and makes a pilgrimage to Judea, I'm not sure what might happen."

"Peter did say that Paul told him he could have the lands west of Jerusalem to preach in. We can only hope that Paul will believe Peter has taken him up on his offer." Joseph said, "But I do think it might be prudent to double the guard here. I'll see about hiring more men on the morrow."

Miriam saw the worried look in her father's face. "I don't think the danger is urgent, Father. After all, a trip to Judea would take months overland and I'm sure boats don't make the trip often, do they?"

"I promised your husband and your brother I would keep you and the children safe. That is one promise I mean to fulfill. But to answer your question, by horse or by boat, the trip there and back could possibly take three months or more. So I suppose you are right, we have a few days before we truly have to worry."

154

"For now, let us enjoy our meal." John said quietly, "Although we may need to find a way to silence Peter."

Nothing more was said as they finished the meal, yet Miriam was not surprised to see at least a dozen new guards around the castle the next day. Nor was she surprised when Joseph announced that he was going into the village to have a discussion with Peter. She almost asked to go along, but decided that would only anger Peter who already felt she had too much standing in the group.

Nothing was said about Joseph's visit during supper, so Miriam assumed that the older man had been able to accomplish little or nothing in reasoning with Peter.

Miriam busied herself caring for her two children and helping Mary spin and weave yarn for clothing. Joseph had hired more than enough servants to do either chore, but both women found that it helped them to worry less if they kept both their hands and their minds occupied.

"Abram will be a full year come the Sabbath this week." Mary said one afternoon as her fingers worked the spindle.

"That is so," Miriam replied, "And Vivienne will be a full eight the next week. Time passes faster than I ever believed possible."

"Joseph does dote on those two boys." Mary said quickly and Miriam knew she was trying to change the subject as she often became depressed when she thought about her daughter.

"He does, which is good. Joshua has forgotten his father, it's been too long, I think. Do you think Yahshua will ever find his way to us?"

"He will, daughter. When it is time. There is a

155

season for all things."

"I hope you are right, Mary. But many times as I lay alone in my bed at night, I fear he will never return."

"Have faith, daughter. He said he would join us here and no matter how much he may have changed, he will still keep his word."

Miriam continued to weave and took comfort in her mother in law's words. She just hoped that Mary had enough faith for them both, because for herself, she was full of doubts. For now though, she would let the subject drop.

Four days later, Miriam was awakened by one of the guards bringing her children into the chamber.

"Stay here and keep the children quiet." he said.

"What is happening?" she asked, her voice a hushed whisper.

"There has been an assassin attack. Until we know it is safe, your father has ordered you to remain in this room."

A fear she had not felt since the day at the quarry pit filled Miriam's heart.

"Who was attacked?" she asked, barely able to choke out the words.

"It is not for me to say, ma'am. Your father will explain all in due time."

Miriam started to demand an answer, but knew she wouldn't receive one. Instead, she began settling Joshua into his bed. At five, he knew something was happening, yet he wasn't afraid, only curious.

"Shush," Miriam said, as he tried to ask as many questions as he could string together. "I do not know what is happening. We will have to wait for your grandfather. For now, lie back and close your eyes."

The little boy did as he was told and was soon sleeping along with his younger brother. Miriam knew sleep was not going to claim her until she knew what had happened. Only then did she realize that Mary wasn't in the bed opposite hers and her heart sank.

Miriam didn't have to wait for her father to tell her the news. She already knew whose blade the assassin had struck. Inside her heart broke and for the first time in years, she felt totally alone.

Chapter Thirty

Miriam paced the room as she waited for word. Seconds dragged into minutes, while the minutes soon became hours before Joseph finally entered the room. His face grave, he nodded to the guard who left the room,

"We must talk, daughter, things have changed here dramatically."

"It's Mary, isn't it?" Miriam asked, unable to focus on any other thought.

Her father nodded, "John found her in the kitchen earlier. She had been stabbed."

"She's dead, isn't she?" Miriam's voice sounded choked as if even breathing was difficult.

Her father nodded.

"Take me to her. I need to see for myself."

Again, her father nodded, sadness in his eyes. "I'll have the guard stay here with the boys. Afterward, we'll talk."

Joseph led her to the small room off the kitchen where they had moved Mary's body. The tears that had been threatening to fall began to flow when Miriam saw her mother in law's blood soaked body.

"Who did this?" she asked.

"One of the newer servants," her father answered, "obviously sent by Paul."

"And the servant?"

"He did not get far. John saw to that."

"I will prepare the body myself. I owe this woman that much."

Her father nodded and sighed, "First we need to talk. Then we'll bury dear Mary. Come, daughter, the others are waiting."

She followed her father back to the salon where John, Phillip and the others were waiting. All their faces were solemn and she could tell that John had been crying. Peter was noticeably absent. She took a seat on the upholstered settee.

"It is no longer safe here." John began, "Before he died, the assassin said that there would be others."

"You actually talked to him?" Miriam asked.

"He talked. Someone in the village paid him to come here. You, Miriam, were his target. I can only suppose that Mary discovered him first."

"But who...?" Miriam's voice trailed off.

"I can only assume he was hired by someone sent from Jerusalem. They know where we are."

"I told you Peter's mouth would get us all in trouble." Phillip said.

"Be that as it may, until we hear from Yahshua or Judas, we'll just have to deal with him the best we can. Maybe now, he will listen to us." Joseph said.

"So what do we do now?" Miriam asked, "Do we fire all the servants?"

"No, we leave." Joseph said simply.

"Leave? Leave and go where? And what about Yahshua and the others, they expect us to be here."

"We go to Britannia. To Glastonbury."

Miriam felt her heart leap, but she still worried what would happen if Yahshua found them gone.

"He'll figure it out, Miriam."

"Yet, we'll have the same problem with Peter there, will we not, Father?"

"No, we're leaving Peter here."

"How are you going to explain that to him? Where are you telling him we are going?" Miriam asked as she looked around at the faces in the room.

"We're going to tell him he needs to wait here for Yahshua and the others. It will make him feel important. As to what we'll tell him about where we're going, your Father has that figured out." John said.

Miriam turned back to her father, a questioning look on her face.

"I'm going to tell Peter that we go to Eburacum"

"Where is that, Father?" Miriam asked, a puzzled look in her eyes.

"I have a tin mine there." he answered, "Yahshua has been there, it dried up long ago. He will understand the message."

"And the message is?" Miriam asked.

"That we did not trust Peter with the truth. By letting him know we're in Britannia, he will know where to find us."

Miriam nodded, her father was right. Yahshua knew well enough that if she got back on her home soil, nothing would keep her from Avalon.

"How soon do we leave?"

"As soon as I can procure a ship for the trip across the channel. A few weeks at the most."

"This is the last time I run, Father. Once I have the boys safely on the Isle, I will leave no more."

Miriam stood and looked at her father. "I'm going home and if I die there, so be it."

Miriam felt the weariness in her body and knew it was not long before dawn and the boys would be awakening.

"Now I must go prepare Mary." she said, before turning and leaving the room.

In the small room where Mary's body lay, Miriam allowed her tears free reign as she began removing the bloodied garment from the older woman's body. Someone had already placed linen rags and water bowls in the room, along with a clean tunic.

Miriam watched as her tears mingled with the scented water she washed the body with. Behind her, she heard the door opening and turned. Phillip's wife, Sarah, stood at the door,

"I'd like to help," she said quietly, "she was a great lady."

Miriam could only nod, and the young woman crossed the room going to the other side of the table. Without saying another word, the two women worked together to prepare Mary for burial.

When Miriam was satisfied that all the proper oils had been applied, she reached for the linen shroud and the two women fitted it around her body.

"It is done." Miriam said, "I will tell the others."

Sarah nodded, "Thank you for allowing me to help. She was always so very kind to me."

"To me also. She was as much my mother as the woman who birthed me."

Miriam smiled. "No more tears. Mary wouldn't want us to grieve for her, she would want us to celebrate her life."

The young woman smiled back, "She would, at that. I know she helped you with your children, if you will let me, I'd like to help also." Sarah pointed at her large belly, "Besides, I need the experience."

Miriam put her arm around Sarah's shoulders, "And I need all the help I can get. When do you expect the child?"

"Not for another month or so."

Miriam felt a twinge of sadness. The chances were good that Sarah would be giving birth either on the ship or on the road to Glastonbury. Miriam knew it would be stressful and decided that she would mentor this young woman, just as Mary had for her.

"Well, then, we'll make sure you're ready." Miriam said, "But now, I've got to tell Joseph the body is ready, and tell my boy's their grandmother has passed to the Summerland."

"The Summerland?" Sarah asked.

"I'll try to explain later, for now, I was taught we just pass over to a better place."

"Like the heaven, Peter preaches?"

"No, nothing like." Miriam answered before turning into the hallway, "I'll try to explain more later this afternoon, okay?"

"All right." Sarah said, although Miriam could see confusion on her face. Yet, she didn't have time to deal with it now, Miriam made a mental note to let Joseph know that some of the group were beginning to listen to Peter's teachings.

***

They buried Mary's body just before sunset. Miriam chose a gravesite in the herb garden Mary had cultivated during their stay at the chateau. The entire group from the village, including Peter, attended the small ceremony.

Miriam found it hard to look at Peter without anger. She felt the blame for Mary's death fell squarely on his shoulders. As she and the children went back to her chambers, she hoped that when Yahshua did arrive he would leave Peter here and not bring him to Britannia.

She fed the children their evening meal in the room. Until they were safely away from here, she planned to keep them with her as much as possible.

John had pulled a chair up outside her door and told her he planned on taking up the guard duty until they were away from this place. She knew he wouldn't be able to be there for the whole of every day, but she felt safer with him than the bodyguards Joseph had hired.

Bone tired once the children had been cleaned up, Miriam crawled into bed with them and quickly fell asleep.

Chapter Thirty One

For the next two weeks, the chateau was a flurry of activity. Everything was packed up once more and taken to the docks to await loading on the ship. Joseph had procured a larger ship than the last and assured Miriam that her and the children would have a cabin aboard to themselves

Although Peter had whined when he had been told of the plans, he eventually accepted them without more comment. Miriam believed that he was reluctant to leave the small number of villagers that hung on to his every word, and although she knew that was an unkind thought, she felt no remorse for having it.

The night before they were to board the boat, Miriam was awakened by loud voices in the hallway. Fearing for her children, she pulled the small ceremonial dagger she carried beneath her robes and went to the door.

Opening the door, expecting the worst, her heart leapt for joy. Yahshua stood in the hallway talking to Joseph. When she walked into the hall, her eyes met his and he smiled, guiding Joseph to the side and opening his arms to her.

Miriam dropped her blade and ran into her husband's arms.

"You've come in time." She said, tears of happiness running down her cheeks.

"So it appears." he said with a slight chuckle.

"I hate to break this reunion up, but there is much we must tell you Yahshua. I'll go tell the others and meet both of you in the salon."

"The children?" Miriam asked.

"I'll send a guard." Joseph answered.

Seeing the concern on Miriam's face, Yahshua said, "Send two."

As soon as Joseph had left the hallway, Miriam stood on tiptoe and kissed her husband full on the mouth.

"I have missed you so." she said.

"As I have you. I could stay away no longer."

"So you will go to Glastonbury with us?"

"I go wherever you are, my dear wife. For now, I just want to have you alone and see our children."

Miriam felt herself blush as two men entered the hallway. She recognized one of the men as the man who had guarded the boys the night of Mary's death. He doesn't know, she thought as she looked at her husband.

"We lost your mother to an assassin's blade a fortnight ago." she began, "I'm so sorry Yahshua."

She saw sadness in his eyes, "I should have come sooner." he said, "Is this why we go to Britannia?"

She nodded, "It is all very complicated. I will let Father and John explain it all."

He looked at her and she could see the confusion in his eyes. "Let's go to the salon, then you will understand." she said. Linking her arm in his, she led him to the room where the others would be waiting.

They entered the salon where all the men, and a few of the women were seated around the room. Miriam smiled at Judas and the young woman he had at his side. He has found a wife also, she thought.

She watched as Yahshua looked around the room, "Where is Peter?" he asked, "did he not make the boat in Alexandria?"

"Sit down, Yahshua. You must be tired after your journey. I have sent for refreshments." Joseph said, "Once they arrive, we will tell you all that has happened here."

The group waited while several servants brought in numerous platters of food and wine. Once they were gone, Joseph rose and shut the massive doors to the salon.

"Where do I start?" he asked.

"Start with Peter." John said, "That's where it all begins, really."

By the time the story had been told and all the questions answered, the sun was fully up and it was time to leave for the docks. Miriam knew she would have to feed the children bread and cheese along the way as there was no time to take to break the fast properly.

As they made their way to the boat, Yahshua stayed by her side holding the squirming Abram and answering questions about his journeys from the barrage of questions being asked by Joshua. The first thing Miriam noticed as they reached the docks, was that Peter was there waiting for them.

She looked at her husband, the unasked question in her eyes. He smiled and said, "I'll explain when we're alone."

She watched Peter walk the gangplank onto the boat, a feeling of dread filling her heart. Trusting Peter in the past had always been hard, trusting him now was impossible. Miriam hoped her husband knew what he was doing. She also knew that to protect her husband and children from the fate Mary had suffered because of this man, she would have no problem ridding the group of him herself.

As she had expected, Phillip's wife Sarah gave birth to a healthy son aboard the boat a day before they reached Britannia. Unlike Miriam's easy birthing,

Sarah had labored for almost a full day before the Goddess allowed her rest. Yet, Miriam was happy to see the joy in the young woman's eyes when she held her son for the first time. Phillip also beamed with joy. On the cramped trip, any pleasure was a wonderful thing to behold, Miriam had told Yahshua later.

She had little time alone with Yahshua during the trip. Although they had a cabin of their own, the boys had been restless and had slept little during the nights when Yahshua would stay in the cabin with her instead of huddled with the men making plans for the future. As soon as they reached Glastonbury, Miriam hoped that the situation would change and they could be together as a family.

Yahshua had changed much, as she supposed she had also, but it saddened her to see the hardness in his eyes. When he would talk about the past, a bitterness crept into his voice that made Miriam want to slink away and hide until he changed the subject to a more pleasant topic. She understood his anger and bitterness though, but hoped that once they settled he could put the past behind them and begin looking toward the future.

They left the ship while docked at Dubris, a small Roman fort several miles outside of Londinium. Joseph felt that if the Romans or any of Paul's mercenaries were looking for them, they would begin in Londinium and they should avoid the large Roman city. Glastonbury was still a journey of several weeks away, but just to be back on her own soil lightened Miriam's heart and as the small band made their way across the island, she told stories to the boys of her childhood on Avalon.

The trip overland was slow, with many stops along the way as children had been born to many of the followers in the time since Jerusalem, several of the wives were pregnant and Sarah had recently given birth. But Miriam could feel the tug of Avalon on her psyche. For the first time since she had kissed her tiny daughter goodbye, she would soon know the child's fate. Was she safe on Avalon? Had Ariade made it safely to the isle? Had she remained? All questions that went through her mind as every step led her closer to knowing the answers.

A week into the journey, Miriam took her place at Yahshua's side after the children had been put to bed.

"Will you go back to Avalon?" Yahshua asked. "It is my fault that you had to leave."

"I shall return for a visit," she answered, "but my place is with you."

She could see his face soften in the moonlight, "I would understand why you would wish to go back. I would release you."

"I go only to discover if Vivienne is there. And to see Cerrah. Then I will return to you and to my sons."

"I don't know what the future holds, Miriam. Things will be different here than they were in Jerusalem. We are still going to have to deal with Paul, before this thing gets completely out of hand. I cannot live in hiding forever, it is not my destiny."

"But what of Rome?" she asked, hearing the fear in her own voice.

"I do not know yet." He said, "but I know I am not meant to just settle down into obscurity."

Miriam didn't trust her voice to speak, so she forced herself to nod.

"I meant what I said, my wife. Should you decide to return to Avalon, you will go with my blessings."

"I will stay with you." she said, her voice almost a whisper.

He wrapped his arms around her and she allowed herself to be pulled close to him. He reached down and pulled the covers over their bodies and for the first time since he had returned from India, she knew him as her husband.

The next day, she overheard Yahshua and Judas talking.

"Peter is still making converts, Master. Among your own people." Miriam could hear the frustration in Judas' voice.

"I know."

"Why did you insist on bringing him here?" Judas asked.

"For this purpose. Can't you feel it Judas? This risen Christ is gaining ground. Neither the Jewish priesthood nor the Roman Empire can stop it. It is all we heard journeying from India to Gaul."

"But it is all lies."

"All lies, but most of all we believe is lies, Judas my brother."

"What lies?"

"Tell me Judas, do you really believe Adam and Eve were sent from the garden for eating an apple? Or that Ezekiel went to the skies in a chariot of fire?"

"Those are allegories, myths; from which to learn." Judas replied.

"And so is the risen Christ. We can turn it into a myth of major proportions and in doing so, turn it to our advantage."

"How?"

"I'm not sure yet, but between the two of us, I am sure we can figure it out."

Miriam was shocked as she listened to the

169

hardness of Yahshua's voice. So he was planning to become the risen Christ, but how, she wondered? Slipping away from where she had been listening, she thought of Mircalla and what she had told her in Alexandria. All gods were one. And the Goddess only had a new face in the mother of the risen Christ.

The thoughts confused her and there was no one here for her to talk to. She would have to wait, and watch, until she could return to the shores of Avalon. Surely, her sister Cerrah, the High Priestess, would be able to help her sort out her confusion and guide her onto the path that she must take.

During the rest of the journey to Glastonbury, she heard nothing more of her husband's plans although he and Judas spent much time with Peter. She supposed they were asking details of this new religion he preached. The only thing she was sure of now, was that life here in Britannia was not going to be the peaceful, quiet life of her dreams.

Chapter Thirty Two

The small party arrived on the outskirts Glastonbury in the early afternoon and set up camp in a large field. Joseph went straight to the Inn to book rooms for himself, Judas, Yahshua and Miriam. He returned to tell them rooms would be ready by dark fall and told John that the Inn had room for few more, if he and a few of the others closest to them desired. Only John, James and Peter took Joseph up on the offer, the rest preferring to stay with their families and the crowd. At dusk, they made their way to the village.

Miriam was surprised when they were given the same room she had spent three lonely days in when she had been forced to leave the isle. At least this time, she would have a bed to sleep in. The Innkeeper had placed another small bed in the corner where she had spent her time on the floor waiting for her father's return. Tomorrow, the next day at the latest, she would return to the isle.

The children fed and sleeping soundly in their bed, Marian made her way downstairs. The eating hall had not changed since the day she had met Clandaugh. She shuttered as she thought about the woman and wondered what had happened to her after her father had dumped her in Alexandria. Miriam went and joined the others at the long table in the back of the room. Immediately, the Innkeeper placed a large bowl of stew in front of her.

She ate ravenously as she listened to the conversation around her, not paying attention to other activity in the room. She was surprised when she heard another woman's voice,

"You have returned."

Miriam looked up and saw Cerrah standing behind Joseph.

"Sister."

"I could feel your spirit returning, I had to come. There is much to be discussed."

Yahshua jumped to his feet,

"Lady, you honor us with your presence. Please sit and join us."

"I shall sit beside my sister." Cerrah said.

Judas rose and pulled a stool next to Miriam.

Cerrah looked hard at Judas. "So my long, lost brother has returned also?"

Her eyes swung around to Joseph. "So, Tin Trader, was the Oracle correct? Did your plans go awry?"

Miriam watched as her sister taunted the old man, expecting to see Joseph rise to the bait in anger. Judas said nothing, only stared in curiosity at the woman in flowing blue robes with a crescent moon tattooed between her brows.

"The Oracle was correct, Lady." he replied humbly.

"Word has reached even here, that Yahshua is the risen Christ. Yet how can that be, when he is here in flesh and blood?" she asked.

"It is." Yahshua began.

"It is going to take over the world." Cerrah said, "The fogs around Avalon are already thickening. Shall I tell you what the Oracle has seen?"

Around the table, each man nodded.

Cerrah told the prophesy of the Oracle and when she was finished each man had a look of awe upon his face. Miriam, herself, sat in shocked silence. Would this new religion, the Risen Christ, rejected Messiah of the Jews truly become the religion of much of the modern world? Yet she knew, if the Oracle predicted it, nothing would stop it from happening.

Cerrah rose from her seat and turned to Miriam and smiled,

"You daughter looks forward to meeting you. I will send the barge for you at high sun tomorrow."

Miriam almost broke into tears of happiness. Her daughter was here, she was safe.

"I have raised her as my own," Cerrah continued, "but, of course, Ariade rarely lets the child out of her sight."

"I would love to see her also."

Cerrah turned to Yahshua, "You are welcome also. I am sure you would like to see your daughter." Again, to Miriam, she said, "Bring your sons also. They can return with their father at sundown."

"I should return with them." Miriam said softly.

"You have been left alone many times. I'm sure they can make do without you for a day or two to allow us time to become reacquainted."

She looked back at Yahshua who nodded, "The Lady's command is my wish."

Cerrah kissed Miriam on the cheek,

"I must go now. Tomorrow at high sun, we'll be waiting."

"I'll, we'll, be there." Miriam said, kissing her back.

Cerrah turned and left the Inn. Once the door was closed behind her, the conversation became chaotic as each man at the table tried to talk at once.

Chapter Thirty Three

Miriam washed and dressed the boys in their cleanest of clothes the next morning. She dressed herself by pulling her priestess robes from within her satchel and attaching her ceremonial dagger beneath the tunic.

"Are you sure you do not want me to return with you this evening?" She asked Yahshua as she ran a brush through her hair.

"Stay as long as the Lady needs be. Who am I to argue with the Lady of the Lake?"

"It will only be a day or two." she said.

"A day, two, a week or a month, it is of no matter. There are plenty here to help with the boys. Go and get to know our daughter again. I know how you have grieved for her over the years."

Miriam laid the brush down, crossed the room and embraced her husband.

"Thank you." she said, kissing his hand resting on her shoulder.

"Shall we go now?" he asked, "It is almost high sun."

True to her word, the barge was waiting at the edge of the lake when they arrived. The boys, while having seen an ocean, had never seen a lake and were curious why they just couldn't walk to the other side. Yahshua told them that while the lake looked small, it was deep and they would drown if they tried to walk across.

Miriam watched as Avalon became clear through the mists over the lake. Her sister had been right; the mists were heavier than she remembered.

Along the shore, she could see many had come out to meet the barge and as they approached, her eyes kept searching for Ariade and her daughter.

Miriam saw Ariade first and her eyes went immediately to the tall, young girl standing in front of her. "Vivienne." She whispered as the bargeman pushed the floating platform to the shore.

"I am home." Miriam said as her feet touched her homeland once more and before she could take the first step, she was surrounded by a dozen priestesses all talking at once. Outside the circle, Miriam heard hands clapping and the priestesses pulled away.

"Mama?"

Tears of happiness ran down Miriam's cheeks as she ran to embrace her daughter. Between the tears, she looked at the child she thought she would never see again. Vivienne was tall for her age of eight years, almost as tall as Miriam herself. She had Yahshua's brilliant blue eyes, and long, wavy hair the color of a summer sunset. Miriam had to wonder how such a beautiful child had been born of her, neither of the boys had any of Vivienne's beauty.

"Are they my brothers?" Vivienne asked, pointing to the two smaller boys.

"They are," Miriam smiled and held out her hand, "here, come meet them and your father."

For the first time in months, Miriam saw Yahshua's eyes soften as he squatted and hugged the young girl.

"I have waited a long time to see you." he said softly.

"Aunt Cerrah said that you were the only good thing in Jerusalem. Was she right?"

"I don't know. But I'm not there now. I'm in the village, just across the lake."

175

"Well, that's good. Maybe Aunt Cerrah will let you visit often." The little girl's brow furrowed, "Although she doesn't let many men come on the island. Can I go play with my brothers?" She asked, looking at Ariade.

Ariade looked at Miriam who nodded. "Yes, go, get to know your brothers."

Grabbing each younger boy by the hand, Vivienne started pulling them behind her. "Come on, I'll show you my favorite place of all."

Miriam watched as all three of her children were soon skipping away toward the Tor. She turned to Ariade.

"My friend, how can I ever thank you."

"I need no thanks. Had it not been for you, I would never of known of this place. I am happy here."

A bell sounded from outside the visitor's hall.

"Come. I think Cerrah has prepared a feast for you." She looked at Yahshua and then back at Miriam, "Now I fully understand." she said with a laugh. "I would have waited for him also."

Together the three made their way to the visitor's hall where Cerrah greeted them at the door.

"Welcome home, sister." Cerrah said reaching both hands to her neck and removing a necklace from it. Draping the amulet around Miriam's neck, she said, "This still belongs to you."

Miriam looked down and saw the amber amulet she had sent to the isle with Ariade and Vivienne. Her fingers went immediately to the stone and her smile showed her gratitude.

"And my brother, welcome to you also." Cerrah said, standing on tiptoe to kiss his cheek. "The Oracle said you would return here."

"And so I have, my Lady." Yahshua said.

"Come, let's eat. We have slaughtered the proverbial fatted calf and are pleased to have you here with us."

They entered the large dining hall where everyone had gathered. Cerrah led them to the head of the large communal table, where honey wine flowed freely and Miriam, for the first time in years, truly laughed.

Miriam kissed her husband and sons' goodbye as the heavy red sun touched the horizon. She stood on shore with Cerrah as the barge disappeared into the mists.

"The mists grow heavier." Miriam said as her family disappeared in the fog.

"The world is changing, sister." Cerrah replied, "And the oarsman is innocently carrying the man who will shape all of our futures."

Miriam looked at her sister, trying to decipher Cerrah' emotions, but could not.

"How can what happens in the world affect us here? On Avalon?"

"The old ways are dying, Miriam. What your husband does and what he represents will widen the gulf between man and the Devine." Cerrah shook her head and took Miriam's arm. "But enough gloom and doom for tonight. We have you for a week. Time enough later for prophesies and musings."

They walked back toward the small house that belonged to the High Priestess. Cerrah continued, "I've had them put an extra cot in my chambers." She smiled. "It will be as we were young and sharing secrets. I want to learn everything about your travels"

Inside the bedchamber, the two women talked until the cock's crow signified the rising sun. Tired, but exhilarated, Miriam joined Cerrah and the other

177

priestesses for the morning meal. As she ate, she realized how much she had missed life on the isle.

When the meal was complete, she sought out Ariade, finding the priestess in the herb garden tending the plants. Miriam knelt down beside her and began helping to pull the stray weeds growing among the plants.

"Vivienne looks well and healthy, my friend. It is clear she loves you as a mother."

Ariade answered simply, "We are close. And I do love the child as a daughter, but I've made sure she knows who her mother is."

Miriam laughed, "I am happy she has had you. Please don't think otherwise. I owe her life to you and whatever you have built together, I will not break your bond. Of that, I promise."

"Are you going to take her when you go back to your home?" Ariade asked, her voice sounding laden with emotion.

"Her place is here, with you. When she reaches full age, then she can decide if she wishes to pledge to the Goddess or return to the world." Miriam could hear an audible sigh escape the woman's lips and watched as Ariade's body relaxed.

"Tell me about the journey here. Did it take long?" Miriam asked.

Ariade laughed, "It seemed to take forever. I never knew the sea extended this far."

"Was the passage difficult? Mircalla never told me all that she had arranged for you."

"Actually, she arranged passage on one of your father's own ships. Of course, he wasn't aboard. Once in Britannia, the journey went smooth. I had enough coin to hire a cart for the journey overland to here."

"I will have to tell my father that he helped with

your escape." Miriam said laughing. She stopped when she saw Ariade's shocked face. "He is a changed man. Life had dealt him many blows these last years. While I still have no love for the man, I do have pity and compassion for him."

"You are far more forgiving than I could be." Ariade said, "So how many came from Jerusalem with you?"

"Twelve other men and their families. I fear Glastonbury wasn't quite ready for the likes of us to descend upon them, but hopefully we will all find a place."

Ariade rose, "Vivienne should be almost done with her studies for the day. Come, get to know your daughter. She is becoming quite a young lady."

"Cerrah says she has the gift of seeing."

"She does, she told us you were coming long before anyone brought us word. Many of her visions are troubling and they give her nightmares. But she is brave and strong. Cerrah believes she may be the next oracle reader when Tamara steps down."

Miriam spent the next few hours climbing the hill to the Tor with her daughter and Ariade. Along the way, the child's bright laughter removed any remaining doubts in Miriam's mind where her daughter belonged. If she did indeed have the vision gift, it would be used to everyone's advantage here on the isle whereas in the outside world, many would use it for false purposes. If that were allowed, the Goddess would surely remove the blessing from Vivienne.

Chapter Thirty Four

The week passed quickly, and while a part of her wished to remain, Miriam was ready to return to her husband and sons. The week on Avalon had proven to her that although she would always have a strong tie to the isle, her place was now in the outside world.

As the barge approached the shore of the lake, Miriam gave her daughter a warm embrace and kiss.

"Mind the priestesses, daughter. I shall miss you." she said.

"Will you not visit again, Mother?" the child asked.

"I know not what the future holds, my child. If it is possible, I will return."

Vivienne, holding Ariade's hand, nodded and Miriam could see wisdom in the child's eyes that belied her age. Giving Ariade a hug, Miriam again whispered her thanks to the priestess.

She turned to Cerrah, "My sister, I shall miss you also. I will think on all we have discussed. And I pray that Avalon will always remain."

"Avalon will survive to the end of time, my sister. It may be shrouded and hidden, but beneath the mists, it will always endure."

Miriam embraced her sister and could feel tears welling in her eyes. Cerrah continued,

"Should you change your mind, Avalon will always greet you with open arms."

Miriam could only nod. Kissing her daughter once more on the forehead, she stepped aboard the barge and as she waved, she saw the isle disappear once more into the fog as the barge pulled away from the shore.

Chapter Thirty Five

The years passed swiftly as Miriam raised her
boys to manhood. The new Christian religion was
spreading across Britannia as many abandoned the old
faith and devoutly became followers of the risen Christ.

Miriam had watched silently as Yahshua and his
followers began telling the story themselves. Yahshua
had explained that by fostering the belief, it protected
them from any harm Paul could possibly hope to inflict
upon any of them.

Only one member of Yahshua's faithful had left
during the years they had been on the island. Judas,
under a shroud of secrecy had left and not returned for
almost a full year. Miriam, although she had asked,
was never privy to the whereabouts of her brother
during that time. Within months after his return, word
reached Glastonbury that Paul had been murdered in
Rome. It depended on who told the story on the actual
circumstances of his death. Several claimed that he was
put to death by the Roman emperor, other's claimed he
had died by an assassin's blade.

All Miriam was sure of, was that her husband
had continued to change. Miriam rarely saw him laugh,
and when he did, she could sense bitterness within the
chuckle. Much as he preached in Jerusalem before his
betrayal, he preached to those around Glastonbury. His
talk of a new God confused her as it appeared that he
had forgotten that, in the end, all God's were one.

After Judas had returned, Yahshua became even
more zealous than Peter in his talks about the risen
Christ. As time wore on, he began teaching a doctrine
that left Miriam wondering where she fit into the belief

system he was advocating. She would never believe that there was only 'one true God' and that the Goddess and other God's were like worshiping a creature he called Satan.

In order to keep the Goddess alive among the simple folk of Glastonbury and the hills surrounding the village, Miriam began retelling the story Mircalla had told her in Alexandria. While Yahshua preached of heaven to the men, Miriam told the story of the risen Christ's miraculous birth to a virgin who had lain with no man. Using the memories of her dead mother in law, Miriam weaved a tale, that while did not contradict her husband's teachings, would raise the virgin to a place of worship only slightly lower than the story of the rejected Jewish Messiah.

Several of Yahshua's closest followers had asked him to silence her, yet so far he had refused saying it only made the new religion stronger in that now, even the women, had a way to follow the risen Christ.

The crowds that listened to Yahshua had grown, now becoming too many to find room for in the house they shared with Joseph and Judas. Miriam had despaired of fitting all that showed up at the door in the cramped rooms.

"I plan to build us a building, just for your teachings, Yahshua." Joseph said, as they ate their evening meal.

"Like a temple?" Judas asked sarcasm in his voice.

"No, nothing like a temple." Joseph responded, "A simple building. A place where we can congregate and talk among ourselves without being packed like olives in oil."

Miriam said nothing as the three men discussed

the new building. She would be relived not to have to serve the whims of those who came to her home.

True to his word, Joseph began hiring craftsman the next day to begin the building process and within months, the waddle structure was completed.

The massive table, with its thirteen pointed star, that Yahshua had built in Alexandria and had been carefully transported first to Gaul then to Glastonbury, was removed from their living quarters and carried into what Joseph called 'the church."

Yahshua led Miriam into the completed church. She was awed by the beauty of the building. The carved stonework that comprised the walls, gave way to two intricately painted shutters covering the windows. The floor was smooth, the wooden planks sanded down until they had a shine. There were simple benches lined up toward the front of the building, where one short bench was centered with two more long benches behind.

"Where is the table?" she asked, after seeing it nowhere in the room.

"Come, I'll show you." Yahshua answered and led her to the front of the room to the small bench.

Without effort, he lifted the bench and sat it to one side. Leaning over he pulled a wooden ring up from the floor and lifted a large section of the flooring revealing a stairway below. She followed him down the steps.

A room, as large as the church above, spread out before her. In its center, was the table. The polished, oiled wood glistened in the light from the oil lamps placed around the room. She counted and saw there were thirteen chairs, equally spaced to a star point, placed around the table.

"What is this place?" She asked, as she saw that

each chair bore the name of one of Yahshua's closest followers.

"It is where we meet. To discuss important matters."

"I see no chair with my name." Miriam said.

"I'm sorry, my wife. But this is men's business. It is the way that things must precede."

Miriam bit her tongue to keep from lashing out in anger. The others had finally convinced him to shut out her council completely. With more control than she thought she had, she responded,

"If it must be, than who am I?"

"You are, who you have always been, my wife. My companion." Yahshua reached to put his arm around her shoulder.

Miriam pulled away, "I have remained quiet while you have destroyed one God after another, Yahshua. Have this your way, but know this, the Goddess will live and you will never take her away from the people. And yes, husband, someday she will rise up once more to take her place beside the God."

Miriam turned on her heel, and with as much composure as she could muster, she climbed the steps and walked away from everything it represented in her mind.

**

With the boys raised, Miriam had little to occupy her days. Her relationship with Yahshua had become strained and terse from the time she had seen the secret room under the church her father had built. Yahshua had begun spending more and more time with his closest followers and less and less time at home with her.

Although she loved her husband as much as the day they were married, sometimes she had to admit to herself that she no longer knew the man she had married. If she allowed herself to stop and think about it, her heart would begin to break, so to keep her mind busy, she began spending more time with the wives and daughters of the group.

She had noticed that Yahshua, while still strong in mind, spirit and zeal, had begun turning more and more of the business concerns of the family to their sons. While both boys had learned the carpenter trade from their father, it was obvious that Yahshua favored Joshua above Abram giving the older son the bulk of responsibility. Like his father, Joshua had become hard and in Miriam's mind, seemed callous in his business dealings.

Yet over the years, Miriam had learned to stay silent. Where once, Yahshua had valued her opinions and welcomed her questions, now he seemed to close her more and more out of his life. Often, as she sat alone in their small house, she regretted her decision not to stay in Avalon when she had visited so many years before.

Judas' wife, Naomi, was a frequent guest, as was Phillip's wife, Sarah. The three women shared the same complaint, the loss of their husbands to this new religion that the men were shaping. The three women were together, slicing apples to dry, when James came to the door.

"Miriam, you must come now. Yahshua is having some kind of attack."

The knife in Miriam's hand fell to the floor with a thud. "Where is he?" she asked.

"At the church. Hurry, we must go."

Miriam ran through the village toward the small

church. Inside she found her husband, alive and conscious laid out on one of the wooden benches. She immediately went to his side.

"Peter and John have gone to fetch a litter," her father said, "but we don't know what ails him."

"Yahshua, can you talk?" Miriam asked.

He looked at her as she knelt beside him, gave her a weak smile, and nodded yes.

"Is there pain?"

"My chest is full of pain, like a fire has been set inside my lungs." he answered in a whisper.

"We must get him home." she said to her father. "I have herbs there that can relieve his pain."

Her father nodded and Miriam heard the church doors open. John and Peter entered carrying a quickly built litter to transport Yahshua. Carefully the men lifted him and with Miriam following, carried him toward home.

Once there, Miriam prepared a strong tea of foxglove and tree bark and took it to her husband's side. Placing her arm around his neck, she lifted his head,

"Yahshua, drink. It will help."

The tea finished, she allowed his head to rest against the pillows. His breathing quickly became less labored and his face began to relax.

"What has happened, Miriam?" Joseph asked.

"It is his heart." she replied. "I fear the beatings he suffered years ago may have weakened it."

"Will he live?"

"I don't know, Father. I don't know." She replied, trying to believe that he would, but knowing deep in her heart that the chances were slim.

For hours, they maintained a vigil around the bedside. As the day turned into night, the men slowly

186

began to leave, promising to return after they had managed some rest. Miriam stayed close to her husband, closely watching his face, searching for signs that the damage had not been too severe for her husband to survive this attack. Even so, she knew that once the heart began to give out, it was only a matter of time before it stopped all together.

Miriam wasn't sure how much time had passed when she felt a hand on her shoulder. Still holding Yahshua's hand, she turned her head and saw her father.

"You need to rest." Joseph said.

"Not yet."

"It will do neither of you any good if you get sick also."

"I am fine, Father. I remember from my travels with my mother, it is the first full day cycle that is critical. I will rest later."

Moments later, Yahshua opened his eyes. His lips began to move and Miriam moved her face close in an effort to hear what he was trying to say.

"I'm sorry." The words were barely more than a whisper.

Miriam shook her head no.

"You have nothing to be sorry for, my love."

"Mary, my Magdalene..." his voice trailed off and Miriam saw the old passion for her in his eyes. She smiled as he closed his eyes.

Suddenly, Yahshua began gasping for breath. His body shaking, his limbs trembling. Miriam stroked his face.

"Can you give him more of the herbs?" Joseph whispered.

Miriam shook her head no. "Only once is what my mother taught me."

Tears began streaming from her cheeks as Yahshua's breath became shallow. Moments later, she heard the last expulsion of air from his lungs, sounding as a child playing with a gourd rattle. It was over, her beloved Yahshua was dead. Miriam collapsed in a heap coming to rest on his body.

Chapter Thirty Six

To his credit, Joseph attempted to comfort his grieving daughter. Looking from her husband to her father, Miriam felt the old resentment for the man begin to surface.

"You should go tell the others." she said finally.

Joseph said nothing, only took one last look at Yahshua and sighed. Then he left, leaving Miriam to begin preparing Yahshua's body for the grave.

As she dressed his body in his best linen tunic, Miriam heard the door to the chamber open.

"Not now, Father." she said without looking toward the door.

"It is I, Cerrah. I felt you had need of me."

Miriam looked at her sister and burst into tears. The older woman wrapped her arms around Miriam and held her close, allowing her to sob into her shoulder. When the tears subsided, Cerrah helped Miriam wrap Yahshua's body in the traditional blue-woad dyed linen shroud the High Priestess had brought from Avalon.

The task completed, Cerrah looked at her sister and said,

"Sit, Miriam. We must talk. I must tell you what the Oracle has spoken."

Miriam sat on the small stool beside the bed as Cerrah walked to the door and placed a small table in front of it, securing the room from intrusion. Hours later, the two women emerged and found the house full of Yahshua's followers.

Joseph stood as the two women entered the room.

"Miriam, My Lady, we have been discussing our Master's burial."

"His burial is decided." Miriam said a new firmness in her voice. "Yahshua will be buried on the Isle, away from those who would continue to defile his memory."

The room erupted into a flurry of opposition, each man shouting reasons why her decision should not be allowed to stand.

When she could handle it no more, Miriam said,

"You stole my husband from me in life, you and your lies. You will not have him in death."

She glared at both her father and at Judas, the two men she knew would be the most vocal. Neither said a word as she watched her father's shoulders slump in resignation.

"You may have your services over his body in your church if you wish, " Miriam said, "but afterward, as his wife, I shall bury my husband as I want."

Many of the men in the room still grumbled, but as Miriam had not been challenged by either Joseph or Judas, their voices eventually went quiet.

"Prepare your ritual," Miriam said, "We leave for the Isle at sunset."

Joseph nodded and turned to the other men. "We shall meet in an hours' time at the chapel to pray for our Master's quick return to his Father."

The men began leaving until at last, only Joseph and Judas remained.

"Miriam," Joseph began, "why?"

"The reasons are many, Father. Some I am not free to share with you." Miriam cast a glance at her sister, "suffice to say, the isle is where Yahshua and I had our happiest days and there I will return him."

"Are we permitted to attend?" Judas asked.

Cerrah shook her head no, "As Joseph knows, my brother, no man is allowed on Avalon after darkness."

Joseph's head moved almost imperceptivity in assent. "We must also say our goodbyes at the church, my son. We will be allowed to go no closer to Avalon than the shore."

They talked for a few moments more before Judas stepped outside. When he returned, the closest followers came with him carrying the litter to transport Yahshua's body to the church.

"Will you come to the chapel, Miriam?" Joseph asked.

"I will await you on the shore of the lake in three hours' time, Father."

"As you wish." The older man sighed and followed the others and his nephew's body out of the house.

Miriam and Cerrah arrived at the lake at the appointed time. Joseph, Judas and several other followers had already arrived. Miriam stood at her husband's side as Cerrah called the barge from the mists to carry them across. By the time they had reached the middle of the lake, Miriam had once again left the world behind and was returning to her beloved Avalon. She could no longer see the men still standing on the opposite shore.

They were met on the other side by the entire host of priestesses, who carefully lifted the litter holding Yahshua's body. Those that carried torches illuminated the path, as the procession made its way toward the top of the Tor.

A deep cavern had been dug near the pentacle of the Tor. By torchlight, Miriam was led down the wooden stairway and into the massive room below. A stone slab, carved with ancient symbols was centered in the room. The priestesses gently laid the body of Yahshua upon the altar. Above his head, the symbol of the triple moon gleamed in the light of the flames.

Miriam was handed a priestess robe, which she put on. Cerrah began the ritual of the dead, leaving nothing out that had been previously reserved only for the death of the Lady of the Lake. One by one, the torches were extinguished until only one remained lit.

Miriam felt a presence at her side. She turned to find her daughter, the crescent moon of the priesthood upon her brow.

"I am sorry, Mother. I know of your great love."

Miriam smiled, yet unable to speak. Maintaining her emotions and keeping them in control both during the confrontation with Yahshua's followers and with the ritual she had just participated in had left her exhausted.

"Come mother, there is no more you can do."

Miriam followed her daughter up the stairway. She watched as the makeshift stairs were removed from the cavern opening. Vivienne led her away, asking about her brothers and other things of the world. When Miriam returned to the site at first light, she could find no signs of the cavern or its opening. Her secret was safe forever and so was her husband.

Chapter Thirty Seven

For days after Yahshua's burial, Miriam remained on Avalon. Reluctant to return to her home, yet knowing she no longer belonged to the Isle. Cerrah had come upon her, sitting at the side of the shore, her head bent in deep meditation.

"Do you stay, Miriam?" Cerrah asked.

"No." Miriam answered simply, "I know my place is in the world. I believe the Oracle has shown my destiny. I am only unsure how to begin."

"As with most things, sister, it begins with the first step."

Miriam laughed, "But that first step feels like a step from the side of a cliff."

"Yes, I can see where it can appear that way. But if the Goddess is to remain alive in the people's hearts, it is necessary that you do what she has asked."

Miriam looked at her sister, who had taken a seat beside her on the shore. "I so envy you sometimes, Cerrah. It seems so easy for you to do what is right."

Cerrah seemed taken aback. "You? Envy me?" she said. "No, Miriam, it is I who envy you. You have known great love in your life. You have had the benefits of raising your sons. Many times I have had to fight my own conscience to stay on the path that I was given."

Miriam felt humbled. She had given no thought to what her sister had given up to remain Lady of the Lake. She knew that Cerrah had given birth to three boy children conceived during the Great Rite; the marriage of the land to the people. She was sure there had been other sacrifices that Cerrah had made that she was not aware of.

"I am sorry, sister," she said, "I spoke without thinking."

"It is understandable," Cerrah said softly, "you are filled with a great grief and now I, and the Goddess, place an additional burden upon you."

Miriam stood, understanding that only self-pity had been holding her here.

"I will go make ready to go back." Miriam said, "I will allow the Goddess to work through me and hopefully live up to her expectations."

Cerrah rose and put her arm around Miriam's shoulders.

"The decision is yours, Miriam. I do know that the mists between Avalon and the world are only going to grow more dense as time goes by. I truly believe that in less than a hundred season's wheels passing no one from the outside world will be able to enter Avalon, we will be so shrouded."

"Will the mists ever lift, sister?"

"In their time, perhaps. But I think many moons will pass before then."

"I will do my best to keep the Goddess in the world of people." Miriam said, conviction in her voice.

She turned and looked toward the Tor, knowing she would never return to Avalon in this life.

Cerrah who saw her look, said quietly,

"Only you and I know who is buried beneath the Tor. That secret is safe until you deem it proper to reveal."

Miriam nodded, the thought immediately entering her mind, 'never.'

At dark fall, Miriam was aboard the barge, making her way back to a world she felt was changing too rapidly and far away from the world she had entered only 30 years earlier as a young priestess of the Goddess.

Chapter Thirty Eight

Unaware of the passing time on the Isle, Miriam returned to Glastonbury on the Sabbath of the new Christian cult. She entered her home to find it empty, which suited her as she still had many plans to make. By the time Judas and Joseph returned to the house, she had already worked out in her mind the best way to approach both on what she wanted to do.

When the sun rose the next day, Miriam was up and waiting for the two men when they entered the room to break their nightly fast. From their faces, Miriam could tell they were surprised to see her.

"You have returned, daughter. I, we, thought perhaps you would choose to stay on the isle."

"I am sure that may have been easier for many of you." she said, "but the Goddess has other plans for me."

Judas' eyebrow rose in a questioning look. "The Goddess has no place here."

"That is where you are wrong, my brother. I believe the Goddess can be here with your risen Christ. And that they can be in harmony."

"Impossible." Judas said.

"How?" Joseph asked, skepticism heavy in his voice.

"Already, the stories of the risen Christ include his miraculous birth by a virgin. That virgin is the face of the Goddess in this world now and in this world in the future. It is her, I choose to honor."

"How will you do that, daughter?" Joseph asked.

"By turning this house into a house for women. A place where women can come to find their path to the divine."

"Their path is the path of the risen Christ." Judas said abruptly.

"What Peter and the others are teaching leaves women out. This is why I was shut out from the circle beneath the chapel. Tell me this is not the truth?"

Neither man answered.

"I will lead the women to the risen Christ, just as you do the men, only I shall lead them through the Virgin Mother. Mary, the mother of Yahshua."

She watched as the two men looked at each other. Finally, Joseph responded,

"We shall present this to the others."

"The others have no say in my decision." Miriam said, "For that part, neither do you. I have only informed you of my plans as a courtesy; I am not asking your approval."

Joseph nodded, "There is likely to be much opposition."

"I care not for their sanction. Unless they plan to plant an assassin's knife in my heart, this is how it shall be."

Judas chuckled uncomfortably, "I do not think it would go that far, sister."

"You may tell them that I, and my ladies, will be of no bother to them. If Peter wishes the women to be quiet in the church, this is the way to achieve that goal."

"When do you plan to begin? And what name will it be known by?"

"It began long before Yahshua died. I had already begun to council women. Now it becomes my full time occupation. We shall live here, and other than good works for the poor and hungry, we shall remove ourselves from the world. As for a name? Call it the

Convent of the Virgin Mother."

"And what will that require from us?" Joseph asked.

"Only that you secure a few workmen to add bedchambers to this existing house and that you and Judas find lodgings elsewhere. There will be no men, from this day forward, entering here."

"For this, we have your vow that neither you, nor your women, will interfere in the teachings and doctrines of the church?" Judas asked.

"You have my vow."

"So be it." Joseph said. "You will receive what you have requested."

Before the day was out, the two men had found lodging elsewhere and construction had begun on the additions to Miriam's home. Naomi, Judas' wife, after much discussion with her husband, had chosen to stay with Miriam. While divorce was not allowed in the new Christian religion, many of the followers had no problem with allowing their wives and girl children to reside with Miriam.

The women themselves were having a difficult time with the terms and conditions that Peter, who had taken over Yahshua's role in the church, laid down for the female members of the faith. As the years passed, young women choose to abide at the convent than marry a man of the faith they were raised in.

Miriam soon understood why Joseph and Judas had been so reliably agreeable to her plans. Now, Peter and the others were teaching that Yahshua had never been married and never fathered children. The cult was teaching that the risen Christ was indeed the son of God and had committed no earthly sins. In Peter's mind, sexual relationships of any kind were a sin against Christ, even though he, too, had a wife and son.

Miriam often wondered if he lived a celibate life or only preached it that way.

For herself, Miriam was content. Her sons, while she saw them seldom, seemed happy and were themselves rising in the church. Miriam did not ask, nor was she told, how they handled the teachings of Peter about their father. In a new wisdom, Miriam understood that was an issue they alone must deal with.

The convent grew, as women from all over Britannia came to learn of the Blessed Virgin. With them, came dowry's, which allowed Miriam to hire craftsman to build a new convent further away from the growing village. The land she choose was in walking distance of both the church and the lake, and when completed, she choose for her quarters a small room that allowed her to look upon the mists that hung heavy over the water.

She kept her vow to her father and brother and never interfered with the growing church. It had, in recent years, become a pilgrimage of sorts, with followers of the new Christian cult arriving to hear Yahshua's teachings.

Peter and the other ten disciples had left over the years taking the message of the Risen Christ into all parts of the world, leaving her father, brother and sons behind to continue the emerging church. The round table of the thirteen was filled with Joshua and the eldest son of each of Yahshua's twelve closest followers.

Miriam was getting older, as was Joseph and Judas. Often the three would meet in the village marketplace. Joseph, who now walked with a cane, seemed frail to Miriam and she knew his time in this world was almost at an end. Judas, too, was not as robust as he had been during the early years and his auburn hair was now streaked with gray.

They talked little about the new church at these meetings, but Miriam knew they had been shut out of the council by the sons and felt compassion for them. Looking into her father's eyes, she could see he now understood how hurt she had felt when she had been shuned.

Seeing the two together at one such meeting, Miriam could not resist saying,

"Father, Judas, please join me for the evening meal at the nunnery."

"Nunnery? What is that term?" Judas responded with a chuckle.

"It comes from 'none wants us', it began, I suppose as a joke, but indeed as it stuck."

"We shall come." Joseph said, his voice sounding weaker than his body appeared.

Those few words began a weekly tradition between father, daughter and son. During these occasions the events of the past, especially the days of Jerusalem, were often discussed. The only events which remained a mystery to Miriam were Yahshua's days in India. Judas remained closed-mouthed about the time and would become agitated if pressed, so Miriam let the matter drop.

Chapter Thirty Nine

From Judas and her father, she learned of the sons plans to leave for Rome. Now in their early fifties, they believed that the new cult of the Christians were ready to topple Rome and spread the religion throughout the entire Roman Empire.

"It is foolhardy." Joseph said.

"The Roman Emperor has declared himself God; I fear he will kill them all." Judas added.

"So who will run the church?" Miriam asked, "Will they turn it back to you?"

"You forget how many years have passed, my daughter. They turn the church over to their own sons. Like you, we are exiles. Although they do allow us to remain, since we have been since the beginning."

"We are respected, yet no one asks for our council these days." Judas added.

"And the table Yahshua built is it still in the room beneath the chapel?"

"They took it to Rome. Table, chairs, even the goblets in which they served wine." Joseph answered.

"So they will not return?"

"They will not." Judas said, "And I think it not long, before all that is left here is us."

They continued the meal, with little else being said about the matter. Miriam told them she was now receiving women from as far away as Rome and Egypt.

"Seems as if they are a burden, the father or husband will send a small dowry and ship them here just to be rid of them."

"Yahshua would have never approved the direction that the church is going." Judas said. "They call me a traitor because I dare to say these things, but all that Yahshua taught has been twisted by Peter and even though he is dead, by the teaching of Paul which have blended in some parts of the world."

"You may be many things, my brother, but a traitor to my husband is not one of them." Miriam said, "I consider them, all of them, even my own sons, traitors to their father and his memory."

"Let us talk of something more pleasant," Joseph said, "We are too old now to concern ourselves with the workings of the world."

"What we started is beyond our control now," Judas said, "It has twisted and turned on paths we did not perceive at the time."

Miriam could resist asking,

"If you had known, would it have made a difference?"

She looked at both men and neither gave her an answer.

From one of these weekly dinners, Miriam learned that Yahshua had been the one to require that each of his twelve followers have a son that would take their place at the star table. His reasoning had been, by keeping the connection from one generation to the next, only then would the council be able to govern the growing church. Now with the elder sons gone to Rome, the younger sons, who to Miriam's ears sounded more ruthless than their fathers, had taken over.

For those not in the circle, these thirteen had begun sending followers back to Jerusalem. When she asked why, Joseph had responded,

"To do damage to the Jews, to those they feel rejected the Christ."

Miriam could only shake her head at this.

"Are they so hungry for power?"

"They are indeed." Judas had answered, "They wish to rule the world."

Chapter Forty

Miriam entered the small waddle church her father had built so many years ago. She wore a heavy cloak and veil to disguise her appearance, but had felt compelled to attend this one service.

Her father was dead, passing peacefully in his sleep three days earlier. Miriam was surprised that she felt actual sadness at his passing. She wasn't sure when exactly she had stopped feeling resentment for the older man and began feeling love. Yet the tears on her cheeks were for a friend and companion and she knew she would miss their weekly visits at the convent.

Sitting alone on a bench in the back of the chapel, she was surprised at how few attended the ritual. A young man, who closely resembled Yahshua, stood at the head of the chapel, with his twelve companions seated on the benches behind him.

He talked of the greatness of Joseph, how the older man had built the chapel, and helped establish the path to the risen Christ. She was totally shaken, when the man whom she presumed to be her grandson, began talking about her father's sin and the hopes that they did not send him to the fires of hell instead of heaven and the companionship of Christ.

Silently, Miriam said a prayer to the Goddess asking for his peaceful entry into the Summerland. Then she stood and left the church, vowing never to enter such a place of hate again.

Judas continued to come for their weekly dinners. Miriam noticed that since Joseph's death, he had lost much weight and his mind had become duller. He became forgetful, sometimes so much so that once the dinner was complete, he would ask when it would begin.

Breaking the vow to herself she had made many years before about men in the convent, she had the novices prepare a chamber for Judas at the back of the nunnery. Here she invited him to stay, to spend out the remainder of his days. In a moment of mental clarity, he thanked her and agreed. She sent several of the young women to his lodgings to collect his personal belongings and have them brought to the convent.

Naomi, his wife now an old woman also, took charge of his care. Miriam would stop and chat with both as time permitted, however Judas' memory continued to slide where now all he could remember were the events of Jerusalem and before.

Within months, Judas passed to the Summerland and Miriam truly felt alone. In the years that had passed, she had truly come to love Judas as a brother. Together, they had been the last of those who remained who had known and loved Yahshua for the man he was. Not only had he been a protector of her husband, but after his passing, he had become a quiet protector of her also.

She sent word to the church of his passing and was angered when she received no response. They did not care that the man who had saved her husband from certain death, was now dead himself. In a simple ceremony, she had his body buried next to her father in the cemetery that had been dedicated to the risen Christ on the communal lands between the convent and the church.

Miriam, at seventy-four still had the mind, if not the body of much younger women. While she rarely visited the village, she still ran the convent with a loving compassion for the castaways of the Christian cult.

During the morning prayers, she was astounded to hear the voices of men in the outside antechamber. She rose slowly, and made her way out of the small chapel. In the hallway, two men stood both looking as if they wished to be elsewhere.

"You are here because...?" her voice trailed the question off.

"We were instructed to come and deliver this message." One of the young men said, handing her a sealed parchment.

"Does it require a response?" she asked.

Both shook their head in the negative.

"Then you are relieved." she said bluntly.

Taking the document, she retired to her own chambers. Using her small ritual dagger, she lifted the wax seal and unfolded the parchment.

As she read, tears streaked down her weathered, wrinkled face.

"Jerusalem has been destroyed by Rome," the letter read, "All that remains are burning timbers and ash."

Miriam's eyes went quickly to the bottom of the page. The letter had been sent from John, one of the few she considered a true friend of Yahshua. She went back to the body of the letter.

"I have instructed that this be delivered to you Miriam as only you remain that knows the truth of these matters. I sit in a small jail cell in Rome, betrayed by my own son. The rest of us, those that stayed by Yahshua's side, have met the same fate. I am to be executed in the morning by the Romans who have convicted me of sedition.

"I give this letter to a jail keeper whom I have bribed to see that it reaches your hands only. I am glad

Joseph and Judas did not live to see what has befallen their beloved Jerusalem. For whatever your father's faults, he wanted only what was best for Judea. I am sure you know this.

"This destruction was brought about the sons and grandsons of us all, working together from both sides of the conflict. They feel that this will insure that, in time, only the Christian religion will thrive and all others will be lost to the winds of time. I fear they are far more power hungry than this and I tremble what the future holds for this world if they ever climb to the heights they aspire to hold.

"This world which has always been filled with upheaval and strife can only worsen if they achieve their goals.

"I am sorry, Miriam, to lay this all at your feet. Yet, I could not let this die with me and me alone. I had nowhere else to turn, but to you, the one that no matter how persecuted, always showed strength and courage. Yahshua was correct, you truly were our Magdalene; our tower of strength."

Miriam carefully folded John's letter and placed it beneath the false bottom of a trinket box Yahshua had made for her years earlier. Now they were all dead and she alone remained.

For the first time in years, Miriam thought of her sister and daughter on the Isle. Were they alive or had, they also passed to the other side. She looked out the small window of her chamber, and though the sun was shining brightly and the day warm, it appeared an even heavier fog covered the water of the lake.

"All bonds are broken." Miriam said.

She rose from her seat by the window and slowly returned to the chapel. In the days to follow, she found her own will to life lessened. She was old and within weeks, appointed younger women to take her place as the authority of the convent. As she did so, she began spending her days in solitude, in quiet reflection of both the past and the present.

Many changes had happened in the world since she had first entered into it as a young priestess of fifteen years. She was sure the future held many more, her fear and what loaded her heart with heaviness was that generations from now, the Goddess and the truth of her husband would be long forgotten.

Epilogue

"That is my story. It is told in truth and love. Many will not believe it, many will condemn it. For now, take it to the isle and keep it safe. When the time comes, it will be found and revealed. There is no truth that can hide under a stone forever."

The old woman appeared to sink even deeper into the straw.

"Tell me child, who is your mother?"

Midraine looked at the old lady and answered,

"My mother is Vivienne, my lady, she is the Lady of the Lake."

"Is my sister still alive?"

"No, my lady, she passed many years ago and named my mother as her successor. I refer to your daughter. The one you named after your mother and sent to the Isle for safety many years ago."

"And you Midraine have you any children yet?"

"Aye, my lady. One daughter, she too is named after her mother's mother."

"Keep her safe, Midraine. Keep her away from this world, lest it corrupt her. Times are only going to get worse for the old faith. I sense that your daughter will become instrumental in the shaping of the future of Avalon. Can you do that for me, granddaughter?"

Midraine lowered her head in order to hide the tears from the old woman she had come to love.

"Aye, my lady, my grandmother."

Midraine raised her eyes and saw that the old woman had passed into the Summerland smiling peacefully.

www.ingramcontent.com/pod-product-compliance
Lightning Source LLC
Chambersburg PA
CBHW070825180626
46818CB00001B/394